L IS FOR Leather

Also by Alison Tyler

Best Bondage Erotica

Best Bondage Erotica 2

Caught Looking (with Rachel Kramer Bussel)

Exposed

Got a Minute?

The Happy Birthday Book of Erotica

Heat Wave: Sizzling Sex Stories

Hide & Seek (with Rachel Kramer Bussel)

Luscious: Stories of Anal Eroticism

The Merry XXXmas Book of Erotica

Naughty or Nice?

Red Hot Erotica

Slave to Love

Three-Way

A Is for Amour

B Is for Bondage

C Is for Coeds

D Is for Dress-Up

E Is for Exotic

F Is for Fetish

G Is for Games

H Is for Hardcore

I Is for Indecent

J Is for Jealousy

K Is for Kinky

L IS FOR LEATHER

EROTIC STORIES

EDITED BY ALISON TYLER

Published in the United States by Cleis Press Inc.,
P.O. Box 14697, San Francisco, California 94114.

Printed in the United States.
Cover design: Scott Idleman
Text design: Karen Quigg
Cleis Press logo art: Juana Alicia
First Edition.
10 9 8 7 6 5 4 3 2 1

ACKNOWLEDGMENTS

Lustful, Lascivious Laudations to:

Adam Nevill

Barbara Pizio

Felice Newman

Frédérique Delacoste

Rachel Kramer Bussel

Violet Blue

and SAM, always.

Words should be an intense pleasure just as leather should be to a shoemaker.

—Evelyn Waugh

Biker style is an American classic.

—Debbie Harry

Kiss the boot of shiny, shiny leather

Shiny leather in the dark.

—Velvet Underground

CONTENTS

INTRODUCTION

LOOK, I'M JUST GLAD I found what works for me. Some people like PVC. Others dream of rubber. For me, it's leather. Oh, Jesus. Leather. I even like the way the word sounds—like lather, but better. My tongue caresses the letters, the way my hands stroke the actual substance. And I'm not the only one who finds seduction in the scent, the touch, the way it feels when you zip yourself up tight in a nice, full-length coat, and…what was I saying?

I'll let Lisette Ashton take over here, with an excerpt from "Truman Capote Was Wrong":

Knowing it was time for her to take the coat, she lifted it from his arms.

Another shiver went through her.

The leather was as warm as living flesh.

As her fingers made contact with its malleable surface she knew the coat would be the fulfillment of every fantasy she had ever harbored.

Savoring the moment, not allowing any distraction to intrude, she brought the collar to her nostrils and inhaled the sultry and distinctive perfume. There was no way to describe the scent because nothing else in the world smelled like leather. The closest thing that came to mind was the feral fragrance of animal passions. The musk from her wet and needy pussy was vaguely reminiscent. But even that inimitable bouquet was not as evocative as the hide she held.

Oh, yes, the smell. The scent of leather is enough to make me stop talking, stop listening, stop breathing for a moment. But then, after the scent, there is the sound. Kate Pearce, in "Sunday Service," perfectly describes that erotic noise:

Leather made a very particular sound when it connected with her skin. It reminded her of an open-handed slap or the application of a rigid length of wooden school ruler to her knuckles.

"Ten strokes to get you wet and five extra because of the flirting."

She didn't argue, lying as she was over his lap, her long brown hair pooling on the straw-covered barn floor, her naked breasts pressed against the fringe of his leather chaps.

And after the scent, and the sound, there is the feel. The glorious, pure sensation of skin against hide. Tsaurah Litzky knows all about that heavenly touch:

He turns me over and starts to slowly rub his gloved hands, his leather hands, all over my body. The feeling of the rough leather at my waist, on my rib cage, inside my thighs is intensely pleasurable. He reaches down and grabs my nipples with his leather fingers, pulling at them at first gently but then more roughly, rolling them between his fingers in a way that sends ripples of desire out into every corner of my body.

Luscious, I say. And like a closet filled with the best leather jackets in the world, every single story in this collection fits just right.

XXX,

Alison

Kate Pearce

Sunday Service

LEATHER MADE A VERY PARTICULAR SOUND when it connected with her skin. It reminded her of an open-handed slap or the application of a rigid length of wooden school ruler to her knuckles.

"Ten strokes to get you wet and five extra because of the flirting."

She didn't argue, lying as she was over his lap, her long brown hair pooling on the straw-covered barn floor, her naked breasts pressed against the fringe of his leather chaps. She'd known he was in the general store when she deliberately got close to Bobby Lee and let him look down her blouse. She'd felt her cowboy's measured stare, knew she would pay, and here she was, letting him tan her backside because she wanted him to.

After five strokes, he slid his fingers between her asscheeks and explored her sex, squeezed her clit, tugged at her already open, swollen lips. When he stopped caressing her and added five more strokes with his folded belt, she bit into her bottom lip rather than cry out. He fondled her again. Her breathing hitched as cream flooded her sex.

"Yeah, soaking wet and ready to be fucked. You'll have to wait awhile. I'm not ready to give you what you want yet."

His last five precise strikes left her gripping her hands together until her nails dug into her skin. Four gloved fingers penetrated her ass and she instinctively arched her spine. He placed his other hand flat on the small of her back until she stopped moving.

She remembered her first sight of him after the morning church service. She'd slipped on the ice and he'd caught her, pulled her hard against his body and held on until she looked up to meet the dark challenge in his eyes. She recognized her own hungers reflected in his dark gaze. Gossip said he'd taken a job as the Holloways' new ranch manager. He hadn't cared that she was the small town's only war widow and that most men put her on a pedestal and saw her as untouchable.

"Sit."

He grasped her around the waist and brought her up to straddle him. She winced as her rear connected with the rough fabric of his jeans and chaps. He kissed her mouth, one hand squeezing her breast, the other splayed over her heated flesh, deliberately pressing her sex against his erection.

On the second Sunday, she'd waited until the preacher hurried home for lunch before turning to find the cowboy behind her. He pushed her up her against the shadowy side wall of the old wooden church and undid the buttons of his long duster coat to reveal a coarse denim work shirt, jeans and a low-slung gun belt. Then he opened the pearl buttons of her thick winter coat and leaned into her, his Stetson carefully angled over her head, his big body aligned to hers from shoulder to knee.

When he touched her lower lip with his tongue, she'd opened her mouth for him. He tasted of strong coffee and cigarettes and his kiss was as fierce and dark as she'd expected. The press of his erection against her stomach made her melt, her sex pulsing and eager for the first time in over a year. Without releasing her mouth, he picked her up until her legs came around his waist. His jeans-covered cock ground against her core. She came for him—even through the layers of her Sunday-best dress, petticoats and panties.

He smiled for the first time.

"Meet me in your father's barn after lunch."

And she had.

And now it was summer.

He lifted her off his lap and pointed at his saddle which lay propped up against the bales of straw. She sat sideways, one knee hooked over the horn, the other over the cantle. Hay poked through the horse blanket he'd thrown over the bales and scratched her back. He stood over her, blocking the light seeping through the cracked walls of the barn. He took off his gloves and, one-handed, worked the snaps of his black shirt to reveal his chest and tight abs. Sunlight swirled around him, illuminating his golden, almost hairless skin, a legacy of his Navajo grandfather. A bead of sweat wound its way down his flat stomach and disappeared into his jeans.

He returned the old leather belt to his pocket. He told her he kept it with him at all times, used to wrap it tight around his cock when he wanted to come hard and fast and think of her. She offered him her wrists and he secured them with the thin rope of his lasso to the beam behind her head.

He needed two hands to remove his gun and undo the big silver buckle on his belt. The one with embossed silver inserts that he promised to use on her one day, if she behaved herself. She licked her lips as he unbuttoned his jeans and revealed his swollen cock. He moved closer and stood between her legs. Holding her gaze, he rolled the belt into a tight coil, buckle exposed at the end.

She tried not to shift her weight on the saddle as he came down on his knees and stared at her exposed sex. Wetness trickled between her thighs onto the leather, a combination of sweat and her own arousal. The feel of the saddle against her sensitive ass reminded her of his cock, the softness of leather over the hardness of the wooden tree beneath.

He circled her slick opening and then slid the coiled belt inside her. The buckle was so big it covered her clit and mound like a man's palm. He tapped the metal; the vibrations spread through her sex and she fought the urge to come. If she climaxed without his permission, he'd walk away.

"Pretty. Wish I could leave that inside you all the time." He put a little pressure on the buckle. "I like to think of you praying with my belt stuffed inside you, lying in your bed at night, all wide and open for me, or at school teaching those kids."

She closed her eyes and imagined it too. Didn't think she'd be able to concentrate on anything but him taking the belt out.

"You'd be so desperate to be fucked, I'd be able to have you anywhere."

He stood again and loomed over her, one hand wrapped around his shaft. "Open your mouth."

He pushed his cock deep and she swallowed him gladly. Loving the thickness of his shaft and the way he filled her with each forward thrust of his hips. She sucked hard, the way he liked it. Her teeth grazed his flesh and he groaned. One of his hands found her breast and pinched her nipple.

The first time they'd met in the barn, he'd stripped her naked and spent hours touching and arousing her until she'd screamed for release. By the end, she'd gone for him, teeth and nails, tears streaming down her face. He'd held her, comforted her, then tied her up and started again. By the end of the afternoon, he understood her better than her deceased husband ever had and she finally understood herself. He just had to look at her to make her wet, to make her fall to her knees and take whatever he wanted to give her.

When his hand fisted in her hair, she stopped sucking. She didn't pull her mouth away from his cock; just let him lie there as she waited for his next command. He pulled out and looked down, wiped her lips with his calloused thumb.

"Kneel up."

She struggled to comply, her bound hands making it awkward for her to balance. He untied the rope from the beam, took hold of her upper arms and maneuvered her until she straddled the saddle. She shivered as he deftly removed his belt from between her legs and knelt behind her. His thick, wet cock slid against her buttocks as he eased her forward.

"Take the horn, honey."

She stared at the bulbous saddle horn, imagined it inside her. He urged her forward, one hand between her legs, spreading her cream, revealing how wide his belt had already made her.

"You can take it. You've taken my fist."

She gasped as the thick leather head butted against her pussy lips and slid smoothly inside. He lifted her higher, angling her hips until she couldn't see the horn anymore, and held her steady.

His cock nudged her ass, pressing until he was inside. She tensed and he squeezed her hips hard. Letting out her breath, she relaxed and let him work his way deeper. Pressure built and her breathing became erratic. He cupped her mound, his fingers wrapped around the remainder of the saddle horn.

"Come for me, now."

Her climax roared through her as he rocked his hips in a shallow rhythm that kept her at an intense sexual peak, so full of the leather horn and his cock, so ready to feel him come inside her. He shortened his strokes, his arm around her hips anchoring her, keeping her chained to his rhythm and demands. She came and he groaned, reached his fingers around to rub her clit, and sent her off again as he finally spent himself inside her.

She remained impaled on the horn as he slowly withdrew, waiting for her breathing to settle down, waiting for him to tell her what he wanted next. She heard him wash himself in the bucket of water she always provided at his request and knew then that he hadn't finished with her. He liked to leave with her scent on him. Her cream on his lips, fingers and between his legs.

Sometimes, when he sat close in church, she thought she caught her own smell on him. It made her instantly wet.

She jumped as he touched her shoulders, drawing her carefully back from the horn. He bent to examine it, rubbed at the wetness she'd left behind. She leaned back against the hay, her legs spread wide, a thick puddle of his come on the saddle beneath her.

He stood up and slowly removed his boots and jeans to reveal his long muscular legs and tight ass. She loved seeing him naked. Sometimes he didn't undress at all, except to unbutton his jeans to release his cock. Absently he stroked his shaft. The scent of the honeysuckle soap she'd put in the water tugged at her senses. He came down onto his knees in front of her and she tried to keep still.

His fingers closed on her nipples, pulling her slightly toward him.

"If you were mine, I'd keep you naked in the house, except for a leather collar. You wouldn't need clothes because I'd just be taking them off you all the time and you'd be so busy being fucked you wouldn't care." He squeezed her nipples. "My come streaming out of you, your mouth swollen from my kisses, your nipples hard. Damn, I'm not sure I'd be able to take my cock out long enough to go to work."

He kissed her, his tongue penetrating deep. "You'd always be either sitting on my cock or taking it in your mouth getting me ready to fuck you again. That's all you'd think about, keeping me ready to fuck you, that's all you'd want."

Her breathing halted as he palmed her sex, rotated his hand in her soaking wet flesh, murmured his approval. Would he fuck her now or leave her like this; so wet she wanted to beg him to take her, would do anything he suggested just to have him inside her again? He crouched between her legs.

"You want this?"

She nodded once, afraid to speak in case he changed his mind, afraid not to show some sign of agreement in case he left her unsatisfied.

He moved closer, framed her face between his hands and filled her with his cock in one smooth thrust. She couldn't avoid his gaze as he stared into her eyes. He waited, his expression calm, and then drew his hips back until the crown of his cock rested at the entrance to her body. His hands dropped to her shoulders. She made a frantic move toward him and he shook his head.

"It's okay."

She almost wanted to weep as he drove back inside her, his strokes long, hard and regular, setting off a series of vibrations as his pelvis ground relentlessly against hers. He didn't stop, even when the climax came, even when she feared she had nothing left to give back. She closed her eyes; let her head fall back against the hay bales. He stopped moving and pinched her cheek.

"You think you're done? You think you climax when you want to and then stop when you've had enough?" She whimpered as he reached between them and fingered her swollen clit. "You'll keep coming until I tell you to stop and you'll enjoy every fucking minute of it."

She came for him again, unable to resist the press of his fingers and her body's automatic response to his demands. He seemed to know what she was capable of even if she didn't. He expected her total surrender and every time they met, he proved to her that she could go further than she imagined. She forgot about the need for caution, her father sleeping the afternoon away in the ranch house across the field, how sore she would be tomorrow—and concentrated on the slap of his flesh against hers and the new plateau of exquisite pleasure he drove her toward.

Sometimes, in the crowd after the evening service at the church, he'd slide his fingers between her thighs and check to see how wet she was. If he tried that tonight, she was so overstimulated she'd probably come. She smiled as he groaned and emptied himself deep inside her.

He'd probably like that.

RADCLYFFE

SKIN-FLICK SEX

LIGHTS!"

The room was suddenly plunged into darkness, all except for the stark tableau in the center of a raised platform that held a bed, dresser, lamp and not much else other than the two naked men crouched in the center of the rumpled pale blue sheets. Blinding white light from the strategically placed stands around the sides of the stage set highlighted their sweat-sheened bodies in a merciless glare. The smaller of the two hunkered down on his elbows and knees, his face against the bed between his forearms and his ass in the air. A burly black-haired guy with a thin pelt of hair lightly coating his shoulders and back knelt behind him. His thick thighs were encased in black leather chaps, leaving his ass bare. He gripped his stiff cock in his fist, poised with the head against the smaller guy's asshole.

"Cameras!"

My eyes hadn't adjusted to the darkness, but I could sense movement not far away, a shuffling of feet and an occasional muttered instruction or response.

"Action!"

The dark-haired guy grabbed the hips of the man below him and worked his cock into his ass. Someone grunted. Someone moaned.

I shifted halfway behind a pillar in the cavernous space and hoped I wasn't in the path of anyone who was more used to walking around in the dark than me. I figured I wasn't supposed to be there, but I'd only come inside to tell the crew that I'd parked the catering truck outside the warehouse. I guess the morning shoot was running late. As soon as I'd heard about this production from the driver who'd made the run the day before, I'd volunteered for the lunch run today. I mean, how often was I going to get a chance to check out a porn movie in the making? *Loaded Leather Lads*—all guys, but I figured sex was sex, and I'd gotten off plenty of times watching guys fuck and suck and blow each other. 'Course, usually I was sharing my viewing pleasure with a woman who was doing the same thing to me, but today I was just going to *look*.

The guy in the leather chaps fucked like a metronome, driving his thick, long cock in and out with speed and regularity. The one on his hands and knees muttered "Yeah" with every stroke. I flashed on an image of me on all fours while strong fingers dug into the bend of my waist and I strained to keep my ass up in the air. I could feel the slap of leather against the backs of my thighs while I took some stud's dick deep into my cunt. Shifting my hips restlessly, I gripped my crotch and tried to ease the tight denim away from my rapidly swelling clit.

"You're not supposed to be in here," someone whispered in my ear.

I froze, my hand still squeezed between my legs. Her breath was hot against my neck, and she smelled faintly of sweet sweat and something else—something that set my clit thumping harder against the inside of my jeans. Leather.

"Don't talk," she said in a low, throaty growl. "Just watch the show."

The guys had shifted position, and the big one in the leather chaps was lying on his back, his legs spread and his dick standing up. His crotch was toward the camera and I couldn't see his face, but it didn't matter—the waistband of the chaps and the cutaways on each leg framed a triangle around his dick and balls like a shiny black glory hole. The smaller one, blond I noticed now, faced the cameras and me. He straddled the big guy's body, braced his hands on those thick, leather-covered thighs, and lowered himself onto the flagpole. His own cock with its wide, black leather cock ring jerked between his legs. I jerked, too, and heard quiet laughter.

"You like a bit of cock."

It wasn't a question.

One arm came around my waist and with the other hand she gripped my wrist, pulled my hand behind my back, and crushed my palm into her crotch. Leather, slick and soft. I closed my fingers around the cock sheathed along the inside of her left thigh and she thrust her hips forward, pinning my hand between my ass and her cock. She was hard, would always be hard, would give it to me hard, as deep and as long as I needed it. She bumped her cock into my hand while both arms came around my waist again. One hand traced my forearm down to where my fingers still massaged my crotch, and she pushed my fingertips roughly into my clit. The ache spread into my cunt and I moaned.

"Unzip your pants. And remember to be quiet."

My breath was coming fast and I struggled not to make any more sound. Fortunately, the guys on the stage grunted and fucked so loud I doubted anyone else could hear me. I caressed the cock and imagined straddling her like the blond in front of me, my come sluicing onto her leather pants while I rode her until my cunt burst and I flooded her. I love the slick shine of come on leather. Hand trembling, I opened my jeans. I wanted to slam back on her cock just the way the blond in front of me slammed his ass up and down, up and down, up and down. I watched him and stroked her cock, the smooth leather a second skin skimming up and down the shaft.

When she slid her hand into my jeans and found my clit, my thighs went soft and I shot an arm out against the pillar to hold myself up. She rolled my clit between her fingers, soft and slow, and I bit my lip. I couldn't take my eyes off the cock across the room, flushed red as it bounced on his belly. She worked her fingers down either side of my clit and pinched. I whimpered. Hurt so nice.

"Quiet," she whispered.

I wanted to come really bad, but I knew I wasn't supposed to. The guy on his back reached around to rub his hand up and down the blond's straining belly, then fisted his cock. The blond worked himself on the cock in his ass in short hard thrusts, all the time digging his fingers into the gleaming leather while the other guy jerked him off. I wanted it to be me, with her cock deep inside me and her jerking off my clit the way she was doing now. She was good, so good. She rubbed the head of my clit with the tip of one finger while she squeezed the core between her thumb and other fingers, pulling and rubbing in time to the guys fucking. I was creaming all over her and in another minute I was going to come in her hand.

Her face was slippery with sweat where she nuzzled against my cheek, and she was panting hard, pressed to my back. I still had a grip on her cock between us, and she thrust into my hand making low, grunting sounds in the back of her throat. I wanted more, so I let go of her cock, yanked at her waistband, and got her zipper partway down before she shoved my hand away. She eased back and I rubbed my hand over her thigh. The leather was hot and supple, like I knew her body would be. A second later she slid her warm cock along my palm.

"Jerk me off while I make you come."

I shifted a little to one side with my hand cupped by the outside of my leg so her cock could slide through my closed fist. I tugged it forward, then pushed back, and her fingers convulsed on my clit. Across the room, the blond cradled his balls in one hand while the other guy kept up a steady jerk-off motion. I fell into step, pumping her to the same rhythm. Every time I pushed back, my fist slapped leather.

Close by in the dark someone muttered, "Get ready for the come shot."

She lost her rhythm then, her fingers clamped so tight on my clit that tears leaked from the corners of my eyes. My cunt pulsed the crazy way it does just before I come. The blond yelled and shot, a milky stream splattering on the leather chaps.

"Oh fuck," she moaned, "here I come."

I let loose in her hand but I managed to keep working her while she shuddered and groaned, her face buried in the curve of my neck, her fingers driving in and out of my cunt. All the while I was coming, I forced my eyes to stay open so I could watch the guys finish. The one underneath yanked out of the other guy's ass, stripped off the condom, and pumped his cock. When he shot, my clit tripped right into another orgasm so hard and so hot I would have gone down if she hadn't been holding me so tight against her. The pleasure jolted through me, and I had to close my eyes.

When I opened them, the room was bright and my back was to the pillar on the side away from the set. I guess everyone else was crowded around the stage, talking and laughing. I shoved my shirt into my jeans and zipped up, took a deep breath, and plastered a smile on my face. Then I swung around the pillar and started toward the group.

A woman in a sleeveless black T-shirt and black leather pants separated from the crowd and met me halfway.

"I'm the production assistant," she said. "Can I help you?"

"I'm the lunch truck driver."

"Good. We worked up an appetite."

I glanced down at her crotch and she brushed her fingers over the hint of a bulge. The leather gleamed wetly when she moved her hand away. My come. Her cock. Leather slicked with sex.

"No problem." I met her eyes and grinned. "I brought enough for seconds."

SOMMER MARSDEN

HOW HE LIKES ME

LATELY, THIS IS HOW HE LIKES ME. Spread out, facedown on white linen sheets. They must be white. No other color is acceptable. A pillow must be below my hip bones, so my ass is positioned high.

He says the white shows off the black more.

"Simplicity is the key," he tells me.

White sheets. Black leather gloves. Ass high. My black hair fanned out and artfully arranged to hide half of my face. It must all be perfect before anything happens.

"You look like a painting," he says.

Charles put me through the ringer until he settled on this. There were lengthy, messy sessions with dildos. Hours of playtime with vibrators. Sometimes the phantom vibrations would stay with me all evening. There were riding crops and paddles. Whips and chains. I spent a day and a half bound to the cinderblock wall in the basement and an entire night chained to the radiator in the bedroom. I sported nicks, cut, bruises and welts.

I was up for it all. Loved every bit of it, to be truthful. I could have gone with any or all of them, but nothing satisfied Charles.

Not exhibitionism, voyeurism, bondage or water sports. Not one damn thing made him get that look. The look I love to see on his face. Where he looks like he's just touched heaven.

Then I gave him the black leather gloves for Christmas.

They were the blackest leather I had ever seen. They seemed to eat the light around them. Little sponges that soaked up illumination. And soft. So soft they were sinful. So light they seemed weightless. They cost me two hundred and fifty dollars on sale at Saks. But I bought them. He needed to have them.

As it turned out, I needed to have them, too.

His face was at first surprised when he opened the package. Then a tad disappointed. Then intrigued. When he touched them, hefted them in his big hands, a slow smile spread across his face. He had just touched heaven.

"Take off your blouse," he said softly. I did as he asked. The fireplace our only light, his face glowed but the gloves stayed as black as pitch.

The instant that glove-sheathed hand touched my nipple I sighed out with pleasure. So good. So soft and warm but cool at the same time. His hands in the gloves were magical. A touch that always felt good became divine.

He stroked every inch of me that night. Inside and out. Any place he could stimulate with the buttery leather was up for grabs. All bets were off. And when we were done, he had that look. He had his thing.

"Simplicity, Serena," he'd said and fucked me, the gloves still on his hands. His hands pressing my face into the sheets.

The sheets had been gray. The next day they were white.

The following night, when he took me to bed, a shiver coursed over me when he pulled the gloves out of his pocket. He set his hands on the white sheets first, smiled slowly and said, "See, that's much better. The dark surrounded by the light. Black gloves, pale skin, paler linens."

I barely heard the words as he started the sinful sweep of my body, traveling every inch of me with the leather gloves. They slid over my skin with secretive whispers. Then inched along my pussy, pushing past the outer lips to reach my clit. His mouth on my nipple was fiercely hot. But nothing felt as good as the assault of leather on my flesh.

One fingertip brushed over the puckered hole of my ass, jutted past the unwilling ring of flesh, flexed deep inside me there. The other hand worked my clit with a steady, slippery rhythm. He made me come. "Simplicity, Serena," he whispered as the vibrations shattered my body.

Now, I know what to expect. He always makes me come with the gloves before he touches me in any other way. Before he fucks me, the gloves fuck me.

So, tonight I position myself exactly how he likes me. Just as I have for many nights since Christmas. Anticipation and excitement lighting up my insides. I would not be surprised to see a soft white light shooting out of my fingertips. I feel bright and shiny on the inside as he moves around behind me. I can hear the slide of his warm flesh into the cool leather.

When he starts to touch me, I hear the door open and I open my eyes. I blink. Confused. A little scared.

"This is Tom," Charles says and my heartbeat stutters in my chest.

Tom is tall and dark haired, with smiling green eyes. Stockier than Charles—wide where Charles is lean, muscular where Charles is ropey. Tom is also naked, his big cock swinging in front of him as he walks toward the bed. He's semierect and for just a second I wonder how big he will be when he's all the way hard. The thought both terrifies me and makes my pussy quiver.

"What?" That's all I can manage.

"I try to give you what you want," Charles says softly, parting my ass with gloved fingers. I relax into the sensation of him touching me that way even when the confusion still swirls in my head.

Then I remember. I remember saying it to him a week or so before. *Sometimes I wish you had four hands. Four hands to touch me with. Two to hold me while you fuck me, two that could touch me everywhere else…*

In that moment, it registers that Tom, Tom with the big dick, has gloves on his hands. A pair that are the spitting image of the ones Charles has all over my body. Tom smiles at me and I smile back. The excitement rearing up inside of me is overwhelming. I don't know what Charles has planned, so I just watch him.

Tom looks over me to the place where Charles is. I know they are exchanging a look. I know they have talked about this. Talked about who will do what to me. And that makes the excitement more intense. It now has teeth and claws and it shreds me without mercy. My heart is thumping as is my cunt. My ears ring from the adrenaline.

The lube is cold as Charles works it into my ass. He pushes a finger into me, smoothing his other leather-clad hand across my asscheeks. He fills me and I'm gone. Gone into the pleasure.

Two more hands begin to roam over me. Tom is there. Hovering over my back, touching my shoulder blades. He slides his hands under my body, tweaking my nipples as Charles continues his sweet intrusion. I realize that Tom's cock, now fully hard and bigger than expected, is eye level to me. I stare at it.

"Go ahead," I hear Charles say as he works more cold lube into my rear end. He can't see my face, but he seems to read my mind. With his permission, I open my mouth and lick Tom. Tom grunts like an animal.

I'm not prepared for the next sensation, because this is the first time ever. Charles spanks me with his leather hands, for now I consider the gloves an extension of him. Somehow, the feeling is softer than a hand-to-ass spank but the leather has a bite of its own. A gentle punishment. The sting is somehow buffered but intense.

I lick at Tom, the sudden pain making me hungry.

"All the way," Charles says to me, "take him all the way into your mouth. Suck him."

So I raise my head and do as I'm told. I let Tom slide into my mouth. I tongue the hard ridges and soft skin of his erection. He tastes like cotton and salt.

Charles pushes the head of his cock against my ass and the fire inside of me grows hungrier still. I swallow Tom mindlessly. My tongue works of its own accord as his hands, the hands of a stranger, take a trip over my body and back.

Charles presses into me, giving that brief reprieve where my body stretches to accommodate. Gives me that moment of calm where my insides relax and accept him. I don't let myself think because the fullness there is too good. Too good to think about the logistics of sucking the dick of a man I don't know, while the man I love watches.

"Good, baby girl. Good," Charles says and I think I might come from the words alone.

He's gripping my hips. He's fucking my ass. He's watching me with a gaze I swear I can feel the heat of on my skin. Another report of the leather on my ass. Another spank. That muffled pain. I suck at Tom for me and for Charles. To please him. It's a messy blow job, noisy and inelegant. Just the way I like it.

Tom has lost his manners and is fucking my mouth. Pounding between my lips like he wants me to swallow him whole. I suck air through my nose and force myself back against Charles. I want him deeper there. I want his leather hands on my clit. I want him in my cunt. I want him to fill me in every way possible but there is only one of him and so many ways for him to own me.

He stops and withdraws. I give a cry, a wordless plea, and he shushes me. I calm.

"Get under her."

Tom does. Takes his hands from me, pulls his prick from between my lips. He slides his way under me, his wide mouth smiling and his green eyes doing the same. I should be sick or scared or ashamed. I am only excited.

I look between his legs and for a moment, I'm just not sure he will fit inside of me. Charles smoothes his buttery hands over my back to soothe me. Tom holds his cock up straight. Gives me a wink, smiles as if to say, *Go on, it will work.* I spread my thighs over him, feel his cock pushing against my cunt and I start my descent. I lower myself down thrilled with the ease of his entry. He gives another grunt as I settle onto him, letting my weight rest on his hip bones. His black hands cup my breasts and his sheathed fingers pinch my nipples.

Charles enters me again. My ass allows him to go back in easily, not having forgotten the pleasure of having him there. And we all still.

The moment is frozen. No one moves. I am stretched unbelievably and the only feeling that shines through in me is a sense of being grateful, completely consumed. I am the one who starts to move. I begin a slow steady ride atop Tom. His cock is not only long and big but has girth that I have never experienced. After a moment, Charles starts to move. I had thought it would be impossible to choreograph—fucking one while one fucked me—but it isn't. The rhythm is off at first and then settles into a perfectly timed dance.

A dance where my head swims with pleasure and my body buzzes from joy.

"Do you like this?" Tom surprises me by speaking. I never thought of him as anything other than a prop. An extra set of hands and a dildo with a body attached.

I nod. "I do."

"She does," he says almost to himself.

"I knew she would," Charles says, piping into the odd three-way sex conversation. Then all is silent but for the sighs and the moans. Sometimes I can't tell who they are coming from.

I see them roaming me. Black leather hands mean so many things—my mind pulls up burglars and bad guys. Dangerous men and evil doings, and my orgasm swells closer.

I have never been full in my cunt and my ass at the same time before. I'd always considered it scary. Now I know better. This is magical. The feeling of two men inside of me. Of being able to accept two bodies into mine.

I'm caught in the sway. One thrusting up into me. One pushing into me from behind. Charles circles my waist with his arms and strums my clit in a slow steady way he knows I like. Closer my release comes, and I grit my teeth to hold on. I do not want to come yet. I don't want to lose this first. This act is new and I want to keep the pleasure for just a while longer.

Tom is clutching at my hips. He yanks me down even as he forces up into me. His hands stop and find my breasts, weigh them, stroke them, pinch and provoke them. Then they settle back on my hips, greedy and strong.

I am pulled, I am pushed. I feel dizzy and free. When Charles's stroke on my clit grows harder and more intense, I know that he is close. He will come soon. I wonder briefly about Tom and then realize I do not care if Tom comes. Harsh but true.

He will, though. I can tell because his mouth is hanging open and his eyes are closed tightly and he's gripping me tightly.

"Serena," Charles says and he's clutching at me as I continue my ride.

Hands, hands, they flit from here to there too fast for me to absorb as he spills into me. Charles keeps thrusting as he comes and Tom arches up, captures one breast in his hand, one between he lips, his hips bucking mindlessly as he tugs and suckles.

I come just as Charles starts to slow. Bright colors painted on the black behind my eyelids. I force my eyes open and watch as the black gloves move over my white skin. Watch as Tom erupts and twitches under. Watch as his black hand clutches at the pure white sheets.

We stay that way. We stay right there. Still. Three people joined until the sweat begins to cool. I bow my head and rest it on Tom who is not so strange to me now. Charles drapes himself across my back and stays there. His heartbeat pounding against my back. He kisses the back of my neck in the way I love.

I feel Tom's cock twitch inside my cunt. Is it coming back to life already? And then I wonder if it's possible that this is how Charles likes me now. If this is how Charles wants me. And for one brief moment, I let myself hope that the answer is yes.

Thomas S. Roche

Venus in Uniform

LARISSA SITS UNCOMFORTABLY in her chair, waiting. She can feel the tingling throughout her body; her entire being is focused, as it is focused every morning, on this single, overwhelmingly important event. It is as if everything Larissa ever aspired to be has become focused on the instant that perfection walks through that door: Venus in uniform.

She wonders if perfection will be wearing shorts today. Shorts and combat boots, so much hipper than the Eddie Bauer or Timberland hiking boots most of the FedEx people wear. But this FedEx lady, *Larissa's* FedEx lady, wears those adorable little combat boots that frame her glorious, muscled calves so beautifully. Well, *little* is hardly the word for them—they're big and butch and shiny and leather, tough as nails; that's what Larissa likes about them. They're fastened with a zipper, just like the ones the paratroopers wear so they can jump into them in a second, right from their bunks. Larissa fleetingly pictures the FedEx lady jumping out of an airplane wearing those boots and nothing else. Oooh la la.

Larissa is fleetingly afraid. After the weekend she has had, if perfection is wearing shorts and those combat boots today, Larissa's afraid she just might spontaneously combust.

Since she took this temp assignment a month ago, Larissa's weekday life has resolved itself into these two segments: 1) 8:00 a.m. to roughly 10:30, waiting for the FedEx lady; 2) 10:30 a.m. to 5:00 p.m., fantasizing about the FedEx lady. But then again, things get mixed up: sometimes she indulges in a fantasy while making coffee in the morning, or sitting there wishing the phone would ring.

If only they'd let me bring a book, Larissa thinks, *I wouldn't be so obsessed.*

But part of her knows that's not true—after all, this is perfection we're talking about here. Larissa licks her lips as she remembers the muscled shape of the FedEx lady's calves—smooth-shaved liquid power formed into a human being. Sometimes Larissa worries when she thinks about those calves—*I mean, the chick can't be a dyke if she shaves her legs, right? Dykes don't shave their legs, everyone knows that.* Except Larissa shaves her legs, but she's only been a dyke since senior year at Santa Cruz—less than eighteen months ago, after all. She's not sure if at some magical point she'll just stop shaving her legs or what, but in the meantime she kind of likes the attention it gets her—out of the office, we're talking. Like she even bothers to *notice* that foul Mr. Becker and his lascivious leers while he makes endless numbers of no doubt unnecessary copies at the Canon next to Larissa's desk. Larissa fucked that sonofabitch up good, asking Janette, the HR woman, about the company's sexual harassment policy while Mr. Becker was in easy earshot. Larissa had been unable to suppress a smile as she watched the guy blanch and make himself scarce. Not a leer since then.

But the attention Larissa *does* like is fairly frequent in coming. But liking the attention and liking the woman are two very different things. Take Susan, for example. Wait, Susan? Or was it Suzanne? Sue? Sharon?

Oh shit, I can't remember her name.

Larissa panics, staring wide-eyed into space as she searches her memory. Susanna or whatever had been a shameless flirt on the dance floor, raw and kind of sexy, over thirty but wearing an Ani DiFranco T-shirt, butch in that not-trying-too-hard way that Larissa liked. But there were other ways in which the nameless chick didn't try too hard, which had become all too evident by the time the sun came up on Sunday morning. "I'll call you," Sue-whatever had said nervously, and Larissa responded with a somewhat bitchy "Right," knowing she wouldn't bother and wouldn't be missed.

Am I just a bitch? she wonders. This is the fourth woman she has picked up since moving to San Francisco in June, actually the fourth woman she's picked up *ever*, her other feminine love interests being entirely driven by dorm-room keggers and personal ads, those love potions of modern life.

It wasn't that she wasn't attracted to the women she'd picked up since moving to the city. The women always seemed so interesting at first, out on the dance floor or pamphleting or whatever, but get them home and it was "I don't know, what do *you* like?" "Whatever turns *you* on turns *me* on," or "What I want is to see you have a good time." How much fun is it to make love to a woman who just wants to make you happy?

What I wouldn't give for a selfish, heartless bitch, Larissa thinks. All this sensitive considerate lesbian crap is getting her down. *Give me a real woman who doesn't give a shit.* Larissa knows she's being too harsh, but if she has to answer the question "What turns you on?" one more time, she's going to put whoever asks it in a headlock and force-feed the bitch her copy of *The Motherpeace Tarot.*

The FedEx lady wouldn't be like that, Larissa thinks. *No way. She'd be the one putting me in a headlock. She'd just throw me down on the bed and do me. "What turns you on, Larissa? Wait, don't answer that, because I don't give a fucking shit. Now on your back, bitch!" Goddamn it.* Larissa shifts uncomfortably She shouldn't think like that at work.

But what else is there to do? Mrs. Fitzwater—"Missus" Fitzwater, Larissa was emphatically corrected the one time she referred to her by the assumed-proper "Ms." (what the fuck was wrong with these corporate people, anyway?)—told her at the outset of this assignment that it was company policy that receptionists not read personal materials during their working hours. "No problem," said Larissa the eager-to-please temp, thrilled to be getting $10.50 an hour no matter what she was doing. "I'll be happy to help out with secretarial work if there is any."

"There certainly will be," said *Mrs.* Fitzwater.

There wasn't. Isn't. Won't be, Larissa is quite sure. Consider, furthermore, the fact that Maclaren has recently upgraded to a new phone system that allows callers to dial their party's extension and reach the recorded voice of a receptionist about a hundred times more friendly than Larissa. Add that to the fact that most of Maclaren's clients are in Chicago, New York, and Los Angeles. Then top it with the fact that everyone, nowadays, has email.

"You must remain at the front desk at all times in case someone dials zero while in the automated voice mail system," *Mrs.* Fitzwater told Larissa on that first day. And, to be fair, Larissa does get a call roughly once every other hour, usually consisting of three sentences:

"Maclaren Industries, this is Larissa speaking, may I help you?"

"Extension 123, please."

"Thank you very much, one moment and I'll connect you."

Not quite as exciting as, say, underwater welding or flying an F-15, the two careers she considered when she was in high school.

Larissa has read the Maclaren Industries employee manual a dozen times, and it wasn't all that interesting the first time. She's sorted the paper clips by texture—no mean feat when you consider that they're all pretty much the same. One day a couple of weeks ago, Larissa did smuggle in a copy of *The Stern Governess*, a nasty little Victorian novel she picked up for a quarter in that thrift store on Valencia—but that caused its own problems, since Larissa only got bathroom breaks once every two hours. She wasn't about to put herself in *that* position again.

"Please, God, please, let there be a bomb threat," she whispers softly, massaging her throbbing eyes.

"Good morning," comes the familiar voice, and Larissa jumps.

"Oh," she says, smiling cheerfully up at the FedEx lady with what she hopes are not painfully obvious goo-goo eyes. "How's it going?"

"Just great," she says, handing Larissa a flat package addressed to Mrs. Rhonda Fitzsimmons. "Just a letter-size today," the FedEx lady says. Larissa squints to get a glimpse at the woman's name badge, but her glasses are still in her bag—and she's not about to grab them and put them on *now;* how obvious would *that* be?

"Thanks," smiles Larissa, doing her best to be coy. She can't see the lady's face, but she's just *sure* she's getting a response. "You don't usually wear your name badge."

The FedEx lady shrugs. "I always forget."

Larissa laughs, as charmingly as she can manage. Smiling, she just goes and *says* it. "Unfortunately, I'm nearsighted, and I forgot my glasses today." Larissa stands up, leans over the big pressboard desk, reaches out, touches the name badge, her fingertips tingling as she touches the woman's warm polo shirt—it's hot out there today. Larissa puts her face close to the woman's breast.

"Jill," she says. "That's a nice name." She almost kicks herself for saying something so ridiculous. "I'm Larissa." She puts out her hand and the two of them shake hands in an uncomfortable, limp way. Larissa's dad once insisted that she learn to shake hands like a man, real firm—probably explains a lot, that—but of course she has never gotten the hang of it and still shakes hands like a girl, which usually isn't a problem but she really hates the fact right now.

"Nice to meet you," says Jill, her eyes lingering perhaps an instant longer than they ought to have done. "Funny you should introduce yourself today. This is my last day on this route—I'm going on vacation starting tomorrow, and then when I get back they're moving me up a block, to California Street."

Larissa's ears ring. She prays that Jill the FedEx lady can't see her face going white as a sheet. She wrings her hands under the desk. She feels about ready to cry.

"Well, see you around," says Jill, and turns to go.

"I'm kind of, I'm kind of—" Larissa wishes she had a brick to pound against her head right about now.

"Yes?" says Jill politely as she turns back toward Larissa.

"I'm kind of new to the city…you know, just starting to meet people. I was wondering…" Her voice trails off. "I was wondering if you'd want to go get coffee or something," blurts Larissa. "Say, tonight."

Jill stares at her, and Larissa is about to spew forth an excuse and a retraction—*I suffered brain damage this morning, I've been smoking crack at work again, I left my IQ in my other skirt*—when Jill shrugs again and says "I'd love to."

"I'm off at five," says Larissa, permitting herself one last shameless glance over the FedEx lady's unbelievable calves as they descend, elegant and strong, into the shiny black combat boots.

"Five it is," says Jill. "I'll meet you here. See you then." She turns and is gone. Larissa suppresses her sudden need to jump up and down screaming.

Five o'clock sharp, and Jill shows up—not one minute late. Larissa almost passes out when she sees that Jill's still wearing her FedEx uniform—blue shorts, blue polo shirt—and those combat boots.

Larissa reflects for the hundredth time that day on her luck—she wore her favorite skirt today, the vintage ankle-length black satin one with a slit up to the knee, kind of hot in a peekaboo sort of way. And her lucky blouse, the off-white one she was wearing at the Lexington that one time, though Larissa supposes she couldn't *really* call it lucky since it resulted in going home with that holistic practitioner. Yech. *Gee, it's almost four a.m.—let's talk about patriarchal body-politics some more instead of having sex, shall we?*

Pushing those thoughts from her mind, she smiles at Jill. "Ready for a cup of coffee?"

"You know, everything sort of shuts down in the financial district at five," says Jill. "Probably best to go to another neighborhood—say, the Mission?"

"Wherever," says Larissa. "Whatever you think." She feels like kicking herself the moment she hears herself say that.

"All right, then," says Jill. "Let's catch BART to Sixteenth Street and go to Muddy's."

"Oh, great," says Larissa, too quickly. "I live right by there." And then, in response to the puzzled glance from Jill, "I, uh, I won't have to walk too far to get home after, um, after we have coffee."

"Yeah," says Jill. "I live by there, too."

"Really," says Larissa, again too quickly. "Fascinating. Just fascinating. Where people live, I mean. It just fascinates me where people live." *I am going to hang myself if I say one more stupid thing*, she thinks. They step onto the escalator down to BART. The two of them descend into the shadows.

Coffee has turned into dinner, and now it's almost nine on a school night. Friendly conversation about love affairs (a nonmonogamous lesbian marriage that ended in tears three years ago, when Jill was twenty-seven), graduate school (just a dissertation and a class in statistics away from a PhD in women's studies when she said fuck it and became a FedEx lady), vegetarianism (strictly on political grounds, and no tofu), vacations (Jill was leaving for a week's worth of hiking in Hawaii in less than twelve hours), and long-distance cycling (Berkeley to Santa Cruz every other weekend for a year now, *Holy fucking shit, no wonder her calves are so hot*) have yielded the nuggets of information Larissa so desperately needs. She's mined the precious metals of the covert agenda: the copper, silver, gold and platinum of the impromptu courting ritual. The salient statistics: Jill is 1) a dyke, 2) currently unattached, 3) kind of slutty, and 4) still the biggest hottie Larissa has caught a glimpse of since moving to San Francisco. But the diamond—or, perhaps more accurately, the Uranium 238—still eludes Larissa: is Jill hot for her?

The conversation turns to such things as leg-shaving: "Strictly for the aerodynamics," Jill says with a smirk. "I don't go in for that femme crap."

That wry smile, telling Larissa that Jill's busting her femme chops. "With me it's strictly for the femme crap," smiles Larissa back, nudging the slit of her long black satin skirt aside as if in venomous sexual challenge. "I don't go in for aerodynamics."

It's over their third shared Turkish coffee, lipstick on Larissa's side of the little cup, electricity flowing through her veins as she realizes she's not going to be able to sleep tonight if she drinks any more Turkish coffee, that she finally blurts it out like the idiot she surely is.

"So you probably have to get up early in the morning," she says. "You probably want to get to bed early," she says. "I mean, get to sleep early. But, you know, I was thinking if you were still up for a drink..."

"Afraid I don't do bars," Jill breaks in smoothly. "The smoke's bad for the lungs. But if you'd like a nightcap, I'd like one, too. As long as we can have it at my place."

Damn, thinks Larissa. *I guess she's sluttier than I thought.*

Jill's apartment is an attic studio near Castro and Twentieth, so tiny it's not even legal, perched so high atop the ancient but revitalized Victorian that you have to climb a ladder at about a seventy-five-degree angle to get there. "How the hell do you get furniture up here?" Larissa calls up after Jill, admiring the view of those smooth calves as she climbs. Then Larissa's head pokes up through the little hatch, and Larissa mutters "Oh" as she looks around at the frameless futon mattress sprawled on the floor and the stacks of books on windowsills.

"Airlift," says Jill, stretching as she makes for the tiny kitchen. "It was a bitch finding a helicopter big enough to lift that mattress. And getting it through the skylight was next to impossible."

With that, Larissa notices the skylight for the first time—high up on the slanted ceiling, wide open to the night air and the encroaching fog of the city as it races by overhead. She draws a deep breath of the night air, loving its sharp foggy scent.

"Sorry if it's a little cold," says Jill, handing Larissa a tumbler filled with ice and booze. "Bourbon on the rocks okay?"

Larissa takes a drink, the warmth spreading through her mouth and throat, then kicks off her low-heeled pumps. She sits down on the well-made futon bed, stretches her legs out and makes sure the slit in her vintage skirt is pointed toward Jill.

Jill sits down next to Larissa, putting her arms around her, their lips meeting smoothly, easily, as if it is preordained that they should kiss hungrily at this very moment with bourbon-bite and the warm mingling of tongues. Larissa turns her head and kisses Jill back, her shawl sliding off of her as her arms go around the FedEx lady. That polo shirt feels deliciously rough against Larissa's forearms.

Everything is perfect for a time—probably, in the real world, just fifteen minutes or so, but it feels like a delicious eternity. Their kisses grow in tension as they recline on the futon mattress, the drinks forgotten on the low windowsill beside the bed. Their hands rove hungrily but respectfully, beginning tentative explorations as if to establish territory—as if to say *I'll get back to you.* Larissa feels Jill's fingertips brushing her ass through the thin, silken skirt, as she coils her legs up between Jill's calves and nuzzles at her small breast, biting the hard nipple through the polo shirt. Those calves feel divine up close, and it's as if Larissa can't stop running her own calves up and down against them, feeling the place where Jill's muscled legs, tough and strong and butch but shaved smooth like those of the nelliest femme, meet the thick, zippered leather of her combat boots. When Jill goes to unzip those boots, Larissa gently touches her wrist.

"Please don't," she whispers. "I like them."

"Really," says Jill, pretending to be scandalized. "A leather fan? A thing for women in uniform?"

Larissa giggles. "No. I just like *you* in uniform."

"Fair enough," says Jill, and goes back to kissing Larissa. That is the excuse Larissa needs to reach down and touch the tops of those boots, feeling the place where leather became flesh and vice versa. Then, as Jill nuzzles Larissa's ear, Larissa hears the question she's been dreading without even knowing she was dreading it.

"What do you like?" Jill asks, and Larissa's spine stiffens.

No. No. Not her. Not this hot, sexy woman in uniform, not this in-control jock, this FedEx Aphrodite, this polo-shirted and combat-booted dreamboat! Larissa's throat seizes up as she runs the question through her mind over and over again. *What do you like?* Remembering all the unsatisfying trysts, all the times she couldn't *say* what she liked because she didn't know, or didn't have anything to draw on. *What do you like?* What a stupid question. *Try me. Try anything. But don't ask me about it.*

But Larissa's state of fear and desperation passes as quickly as it came, as she feels the smoothness of those leather boots under her fingertips. She throws it to the wind.

"I'll show you what I like," says Larissa wickedly, and disappears between Jill's legs.

"Oh my God," says Jill, wide-eyed in the darkness.

Larissa starts by running her tongue around the tops of those boots, her tongue-tip flickering from flesh to leather and back again. Jill is wearing low socks, so there's no pesky cotton to get in between the two fetish-fabrics of Larissa's choice, skin and flesh. Then, as her excitement mounts, Larissa licks her way down the side of those well-polished boots, one hand snaking slowly up Jill's leg as the other hand caresses the upper. Larissa is shocked at herself—she's never taken control like this, and it feels especially weird to be taking control by licking this girl's boots but then again, this is exactly what she's fantasized about a hundred or a thousand times while sitting at her desk at Maclaren, the memory of these glorious calves filling her mind: licking these boots, fondling these glorious calves. How odd that she would have to take control so firmly to enjoy this gesture of submission—or *is* it a gesture of submission?

Larissa doesn't give a fuck anymore. She starts licking the upper, surprised at how rough the well-polished leather feels under her tongue. Her hand trails up Jill's leg, caressing the gorgeous calves, but each time inching higher, further up Jill's body, as Jill sighs and moans softly with each caress of Larissa's fingertips on her inner thighs. God, Larissa can't even believe she's doing it—but there she is. Her hand's sliding up Jill's pant leg, sliding deep into those mysterious, hallowed shorts. Exploring the curves of Jill's upper thigh, and delving deeper—

Larissa almost curses. Jill is wearing biking shorts as underwear. *What did I expect*? Larissa wonders. *A G-string? Hardly workaday wear…* Then Larissa remembers that she, in fact, is wearing a G-string under the silk skirt, so maybe it wouldn't have been that out of the ordinary. But it wouldn't have suited Jill's idiom, would it?

Larissa manages to do what she does almost without missing a beat. She has to, because if she pauses, then Jill will notice that her hands are shaking. She reaches up to Jill's belt, and unfastens it with one hand. Jill just watches—doesn't move to help, the way Larissa's other recent lovers have. Doesn't interfere with the magic to be had, the succulent feeling of undressing a lover. Larissa's tongue is still resting against the leather of Jill's boot as she reaches up and draws the zipper of her shorts down, grabs hold of the belt and the waistband of Jill's bike shorts and, with a single movement smoother than Larissa would have dreamed possible, pulls off the whole mess in one gesture.

Larissa's fingertips rest lazily against Jill's pubic hair as she licks her way one last time around those gorgeous calves in their black-leather sheath, and then licks her way up Jill's legs—passing the sharp scent of her sex, saving that for later—and wriggles fully atop Jill, hands sliding up under the polo shirt.

Then the kisses again, fiercer and harder than before, like Jill is trying to eat Larissa in one bite. Larissa goes wet to the knees.

With minimal struggle they get Jill's polo shirt off, and discard it atop the growing pile of clothes next to the bed. Then comes the tiny little sports bra—double-A, and lucky Larissa, she's always had a thing for women with small tits. Then it's Larissa's turn, Jill's hands surer than they were before, confidence gained from the taste of leather on her lover's tongue. Larissa's lucky blouse, then her skirt, mingling with Jill's shorts and polo shirt and bra on the floor. Then off comes Larissa's little half-slip, her bra, her little G-string before Larissa even knows what's happening. She can feel the lustful tension in Jill's impressive muscles, feel the demands pulsing through that taut, athletic body. There will be no more *What do you likes* tonight, Larissa knows, but she's hardly prepared for the tangling passion in Jill's limbs as she pushes Larissa onto her back and takes a quick slug of bourbon for a purpose Larissa doesn't realize until she feels that ice-cold tongue on her clit and shrieks, then shudders and moans as it traces a path from clit to cunt and tenderly moves around her labia, the ice cooling her but quickly melting as Larissa's heat rises. Then it's just molten lust and Jill's tongue, wriggling its way into Larissa, exploring the realms of those earlier *I'll get back to yous*.

Larissa looks down to see Jill hunched on hands and knees over her, face buried in her thighs, pillow wedged under Larissa's ass—*How the hell did that pillow get there?*—and Jill's gorgeous calves taut with muscle, framed, as before, in those lovely, sexy combat boots. But even as Larissa climaxes, it's not the combat boots she sees, though that's what she's looking at—it's the concentration in Jill's eyes, about all

Larissa can see of the FedEx lady's face, the passionate intensity in those sparkling baby-blues as Jill's mouth wrestles and plays with cunt and clit. The top of Jill's tongue finally drives Larissa over the top, making her whole body shudder and squirm with orgasm as the tainted tongue returns to her clit and pushes her past the brink.

It's a long time later—almost dawn, in fact—when Larissa awakes after an hour-long nap to see the FedEx lady dressed again. Jill's face is scrubbed and pink from a hot shower in this predawn chill. She's no longer wearing a polo shirt or walking shorts—she's got on a bright blue T-shirt with the sleeves cut off and a blue sports bra underneath, black spandex biking shorts, and Timberland hiking boots. Her backpack is next to the "door"—really more of a hatch.

"Sleep as long as you want," Jill tells Larissa, leaning down as Larissa rolls over, the damp white sheet clinging to her naked body. Jill kisses Larissa on the mouth, and Larissa just stares, smiling, unable to believe she just made it with this vision of perfection, with Venus in uniform. "Just close the garage door downstairs when you leave. It locks automatically."

"Thanks," says Larissa. "I have to get to work soon, anyway. When do you get back?"

"A week from tomorrow," says Jill.

"You going to call me?" Larissa's almost holding her breath as she asks that one.

"Maybe," says Jill with a mischievous smirk, and Larissa breathes more easily. A "sure, of course" would have meant a definite no. And a "maybe" meant "maybe," which Larissa could deal with. "Maybe I'll just drop by one afternoon," Jill adds with a wicked look, and Larissa smiles.

"I'd like that," she says.

Then there's one more kiss, and Jill is gone, down the hatch that leads to the garage that leads to the street. And Larissa is rolling over, twined in Jill's sheets, inhaling deeply of the FedEx lady's scent. She has to masturbate three times to get herself to leave, and she's twenty minutes late to work.

There must be some sort of lesson here, Larissa thinks to herself as she hands the single outgoing FedEx to the buffed-up guy who has replaced Jill on the route. Except Larissa can't figure, even with her hours and hours of empty time to think about it, what the lesson is supposed to be. Something about asking for what she wants, or, more likely, something about shorts and leather combat boots? Larissa can't see how it really matters.

She never does confirm it—how could she, really?—but Larissa is pretty sure *Mrs.* Fitzwater decides to get rid of her just that day, because of the doodling thing. Fitzwater just happens to walk up when Larissa is doodling absently on the desk blotter—drawing a woman in a FedEx uniform, a suspiciously tight FedEx uniform, with walking shorts and knee-high combat boots. Larissa reddens at the time, but later she takes a certain pleasure at having freaked the old bitch out enough to get herself fired. *I mean, grow up, huh?* Larissa gets her call from the temp agency that afternoon—*Maclaren Industries no longer needs a receptionist.*

But Larissa must have someone looking out for her—Venus, maybe, nestled comfortably at 35,000 feet between here and Hawaii, wearing hiking boots and a pair of too-tight biking shorts, casting spells of love down upon San Francisco's mortals. Because, wouldn't you know it? The temp agency has just gotten a call for another position, this one in the mailroom of a nonprofit, where it will be Larissa's duty to handle all outgoing shipments through all couriers—including the USPS and FedEx.

The job doesn't pay that well, since it's for a nonprofit—on California Street. Larissa thinks she probably says yes too fast, sounding desperate. But she doesn't want some cruel twist of fate to sever the phone line or otherwise take away the job before she can accept.

She doesn't mind the cut in pay. Besides, now she can wear jeans to work. Or shorts.

Larissa carefully folds her drawing, tucks it into her purse, and with a cheerful "See you, *Mizzzz* Fitzwater," bids the biddy good-bye.

SHERI GILMORE

CLEANUP ON AISLE TEN

"LISTEN."

My gaze followed the voice, rich and commanding, but quiet.

"Come help me," he said, dropping one hand, slowly.

I watched in fascination as his fingers brushed across his crotch then rested at his thigh. The bulge evident through the denim hinted at deviant pleasures. My mouth went dry. "What with?"

He smiled and held up a large leather dog collar and a metal leash. "There's not a price on any of this back there."

I exhaled slowly. The imaginary sensation of the collar pulling tight around my throat as this man led me around his bed, alternately spanking me with the wide leather belt that hugged his lean hips, flashed through my mind. Shaking my head, I took the items from him and noticed that my palms were damp.

Our fingers brushed. The quiver of desire that shot down my back to my clit forced me to take a hard swallow. I tried to stay focused on my job and not—my gaze shot to his crotch—his cock, cupped lovingly by all that dark denim. I glanced sharply at his face. His smile was wicked hot, almost to the point of feral. His eyes were open wide and intense with dilated pupils—focused entirely on me.

"There's usually a bar code on these or on the shelf below." I felt like one of those African gazelles, prey to a more dominant species.

"Show me."

My stomach did all kinds of flip-flops at those two words. He wasn't asking; he was telling, challenging me. I should have rebelled, instantly. His type always got me into trouble.

When he stepped back to indicate that I should come out from behind the safety of my cube, I knew that if I did what he commanded I'd be willingly submitting to him.

And what's more, he knew it, too.

It was a game, one with unspoken rules, but I knew exactly what he was saying by bringing that collar and chain to me. Everything, except what type of punishment would be meted out if I broke any little rule. I bit the inside of my mouth, trying to consider all the possible scenarios.

Did I want to play with this man bad enough to risk losing my job? Was this guy any different than my usual mistake, or did he just dress better?

My gaze slid over his pressed jeans and neatly tucked-in T-shirt.

The clock on the wall in the back of the store *ticked* loudly, blending with the beating of my heart and his steady breath, in and out. It was just him and me—no one else.

Something glass shattered in the aisle across from my register, snapping me out of the strange time warp. I automatically reached for my microphone. "Cleanup on aisle five, Jimmy."

I pushed the mike away, but hesitated, glancing away from the man, who patiently waited for me. Clearing my throat, I pulled the microphone back to my lips. "Cindy, open on register two, please. Open on register two."

Cindy walked quickly to the register next to mine, mumbling about having her lunch break interrupted. She pursed her lips and rolled her gaze to the ceiling. "Do I need to check that guy out?"

I didn't look at *the guy*. Stepping out of my stall, I closed the gate with a *snap*. "No, he's got a cleanup on aisle"—my gaze wandered to the collar—"ten. I'll take care of it, then I'm taking lunch."

I squeezed between him and the counter, noticing he didn't bother giving me any additional room to maneuver past him. "Excuse me..." I said, not meeting his gaze, as I eased by him, "...Sir." The scrape of my breasts across the front of his T-shirt forced my nipples to tingle and draw into tight pebbles.

"Christopher," he whispered in a husky voice. "*Sir* Christopher."

I watched his knuckles tighten around the chain and I bit my lip. When I'd walked about a foot past him, he wrapped a hand around my upper arm. Everything within me stilled. I waited to see what he would instruct me to do. I wanted to feel that collar around my throat. I wanted it so bad that I could almost feel the cold of the chain wrapped tight around my wrists and ankles, tugging my legs farther apart so he could enter me from behind.

Quickly scanning the store mirrors, I noticed customers on almost every aisle. How we were going to escape discovery by Herb, my manager? His number one rule was Don't Date the Customers.

Christopher's nose tunneled into my hair just above my ear. The warmth of his breath caused spirals of pleasure along my neck and spine. Any thoughts or worries of Herb faded.

"Say my name." He squeezed my arm where he held me.

"Sir Christopher."

He kissed my hair and released me, allowing me to lead the way to the hardware aisle—aisle ten.

It was so ironic that I almost laughed. In all the years I had worked here at the QFC, I had never caught anyone fucking or screwing around on this aisle. We got a lot of weirdos, being adjacent to Key Arena. The fact that I was going to be the first culprit had me grinning.

Actually, I was on the verge of laughing, but the guy I wanted to fuck would think I was crazy, and I could hear Herb in the bread section scolding some kids for "squeezing the merchandise."

A firm, warm hand smoothed over my hip.

My stance wavered; his hold tightened. I closed my eyes in an attempt to squash the sensations dancing through my nerve endings and settling in my clit. At that moment he could have done anything he wanted to me. I was his. Shaking my head, I opened my eyes and continued down the aisle, concentrating on the items on the shelves—lightbulbs, batteries, duct tape...hmm, that could come in handy. Ah, pet supplies.

Feeling the heat of his body close to mine, I was very conscious of the others present just a couple of aisles over. If Herb caught me with this guy, I was history. I cleared my throat, trying to regain my perspective instead of being seduced so easily by a hot body, a pair of blue eyes, and some unspoken promise of ecstasy that never lasted beyond the moment of climax.

"Here we are…Sir." Facing the shelf, I scanned for a price or bar code, but surprisingly there was none. "Wow, there really isn't a price listed."

"That is what I told you," he said. Sarcasm and humor wormed its way through his words. He leaned closer.

I turned and studied him for the first time since leaving my stall. The fluctuating confusion and excitement I felt dazed me a bit. "You really want to buy a collar and a leash?"

"Yes." The eyebrow rose again. "If I'm going to use them, I thought it best if I bought them first."

"Exactly what are you going to use them for?" I asked, trying to get some control over this situation.

Watching me closely, he crossed his arms over his chest and leaned a shoulder against the shelf. "I'm going to put *my* collar on you along with *my* leash. When I bend you over that shelf I will control your movements while I fuck you from behind." He stepped closer; his breath fanned hot across my cheek. "Then, if I like you well enough I'm going to fuck you again tomorrow night, and the next."

"Why?" I asked, barely getting the words out. While my throat had gone dry at the image of his words, my pussy was soaking wet.

"I like the way you always greet me whenever I come in here." He tugged at a strand of my hair. "In fact, I want to hear you greet me again." His grip tightened, turning the playful tug into a painful pull.

I cleared my throat and said, "Welcome to QFC. We…I…offer service with a smile."

White teeth flashed in the most heart-stopping smile. "I don't see a smile." He laughed, touching the leather leash-handle to my nose.

I grinned. He leaned closer, brushing his lips across mine. "You're cute, you know that? I always thought you'd be fun to play with."

My heart turned a somersault at the touch of his mouth on mine. When he pulled away, I licked my lips. I've always been game for sexual adventures, but not with such high stakes attached. Still, I didn't protest when he lifted my arms and pulled the smock over my head. When the sweater loosened from my pants I stood there, silent as a little mouse, and watched his hands work swiftly and expertly.

His fingertips skimmed across my skin as he unbuttoned my jeans.

The muscles in my abdomen quivered. I grabbed his hands. "Wait, wait. Let's slow this down a bit."

Glancing up and down the aisle in case anyone was near, I fought to get a grip on my rising libido, so I could scope the terrain. "We can't do anything here."

He sighed, turning his hands within mine to clasp my wrists. He moved my arms behind me, bringing me close into the heat of his body. Angling his head, his mouth explored the curve of my neck. "I like playing on the very edge, where everyone can see. That's the fun."

I didn't struggle; I couldn't. His words had zoomed in on one of my most erogenous zones—my mind. In a matter of minutes this stranger had done what all my past lovers hadn't been able to. He was amazing.

A hard bite from his teeth was followed by a lick from a very warm, wet tongue.

"Jesus." I groaned as my knees buckled. Kiss my neck the right way and I'm your prisoner for life.

He pushed me against the shelf, then wrapped my fingers around the edge of the metal. Merchandise scattered, falling to the floor with a clatter. A dog toy squeaked beneath my tennis shoe. "Hold on and don't let go until I tell you no matter what or who happens down this aisle. Understand?"

I nodded, hearing the promise of punishment if I disobeyed. I shuddered. Not in fear, but excitement. "D-do you like to spank your playmates?" I asked, not caring if I was on the verge of begging. That was one of the joys of submission; I could beg all I wanted. The only downside was that my Dominant could give me what I wanted, or decide I needed something entirely different.

"Only bad little cashiers who don't follow instructions the way they are supposed to," he whispered, unzipping my jeans and pulling them down around my ankles with one swift tug.

My pussy lips swelled, growing slicker by the second. His thumb and forefinger tore my undies from between my legs and threw them onto the floor.

"You won't need those anymore tonight."

A long finger smoothed between the slit of my pussy. Throwing my head back, I gripped the metal counter tighter and angled my hips into his stroke. "Oh, yeah."

"Call me 'Sir' just like the good little server you offered to be when I walked in." He removed the stimulation. "Understand?"

I nodded.

"I can't hear you."

"Yes, Sir." I watched him tear the product tags off the collar and leash.

Sir Christopher. Such a gentleman on the outside, but inside where it counted he was a master of kink, royalty at its finest. Like an artist, he studied his handiwork, intent in his concentration. Wrapping the leather around my throat, tightening the strap into the snuggest position, he placed the metal buckle and identification bracket cool against my skin. He stepped back. "You're perfect."

I swallowed against the unfamiliar pressure of the collar. A tiny moment of suffocation forced my heartbeat and breathing to increase.

With firm, sure fingers he stroked through my hair and over my face. "It's okay, baby. You can breathe. Just relax."

I took several deep breaths, releasing the oxygen from my lungs in moderated puffs. Slowly, the anxiety receded.

He kissed my forehead. "Ready to continue?"

I nodded.

Next came the leash. Out of the package, it was over six feet long. He clipped the leash clasp onto the collar's metal loop. The excess chain rattled against the floor.

"It's too long," I said.

"Not for what I'm going to do." A quick wink accompanied a playful grin. "Turn around."

Facing the emptied shelves, I kept my hands clasped around the edge of the metal, as he'd instructed. The length of the leash danced against the sensitive skin of my inner thighs and brushed the hair of my pussy. I shivered.

The desire to have the cold metal rubbing intimately against my clit and between the outer folds of my pussy rose within my imagination. I closed my eyes and leaned my forehead against my hands.

The collar pulled, as the chain tightened between my breasts and along the length of my torso. Sir Christopher drew the excess length slowly along my pussy between my legs, tightening and releasing the metal to create a torturing sawing motion across my clit. I sighed.

He knew exactly what I needed. When he wrapped the excess chain around his left hand and wrist, I gasped and gripped the shelf so hard my fingers felt like they would break. Sweat peppered my forehead as I worked my hips forward and back in opposition to the chain's motion. With the added friction, the juices ran freely from my pussy, coating the inside of my thighs.

"Put your hands on the lower shelf and offer yourself to me."

I did as he instructed, feeling warm fingers stroke up my thighs and over my bared ass several times. All the while, Sir Christopher worked the chain up and around my sensitive flesh. Finally, he pushed me forward where my bared boobs lay flush against the metal shelving. My nipples tightened with the sudden cold; my clit throbbed with renewed heat. "Please—"

"What?" he asked, leaning his weight against me. The rough denim of his jeans produced an entirely new source of stimulation behind me. He bit my lower back.

I groaned, giving myself over to the moment of tactile pleasure attacking my entire body.

The chain snapped hard and tight across my clit.

I whimpered, but moisture flooded anew from my cunt with the pleasure of that exquisite pain. "Fuck me."

Smack! His palm resounded against my ass. "Wrong. Try again."

I jumped, jerking my head up. The chain pulled so tight that the metal felt as if it was cutting into me. I swallowed the cry of pain that rose and whispered, "Please fuck me, Sir."

A zipper sounded behind me and there was a swoosh of air and the sound of material sliding over skin. "Good girl."

The searing heat of his cock rubbed between my asscheeks. "Is this what you want?"

I nodded, then remembered my stinging skin. "Yes, Sir."

He positioned the chain tight from my neck to against my clit. The excess dangled and tickled along my crevice.

I had a second to wonder why he held it so loose when he must know I wanted—

"Oh fuck!" I clawed for support with my fingers along the back of the shelf, as he pushed his cock into my body along with the length of slackened chain.

Sir Christopher's cock alone would have been enough to send me over the edge, but with the added stimulation of the thick cold metal, I stood rigid and panted with each thrust he made. His hands grasped either side of my hips.

As he pumped into my cunt, he guided and positioned me where he wanted. The chain not only offered the most exquisite pleasure within my body; outside it restrained and controlled how I responded to his every move. Every time I angled my head up, Sir Christopher tightened his grip, pulling my head back into a submissive posture.

I wanted to scream. My orgasm was gaining momentum and I needed to move. The restraint he placed upon me brought an upsurge of anger. I jerked my head and shoulders hard, breaking the hold he exerted.

All motion halted. Sir Christopher stood perfectly still behind me.

My breaths were staggered and ragged, as if I were recovering from a hard cry. Finally, after several seconds they subsided and I stood as still as he.

"Are you ready to resume, or should we cancel this exercise?"

I snorted, resenting his tone. "Sounds like you're talking to some bitch you're out walking for the first time."

He leaned down, placing his mouth close to my ear. "I am."

Three sharp, stinging smacks to my ass brought tears anew to my eyes. I could feel his cock easing from my body. "No! Please…"

He stopped; my pussy clenched and released, trying to pull his length back into the aching void he left behind. "Please what?"

My body shook with reaction and humiliation, but I lowered my head in submission. "Please continue fucking me, Sir."

He pulled the chain and inched back into me a fraction. "If you pull away again, I will make you wait a few nights before we attempt another *walk in the park*. Understand?"

"Yes, Sir." I lay flush against the metal shelf and offered my ass in appeasement. I swear I saw stars as he pushed all the way into my body. The feel of several loops of the chain wrapped around the length of his cock rammed into me, hard and fast. My head smacked against the back of the shelving unit. I vaguely heard items on the other side sliding and shifting with each impact. I didn't care as long as he fucked me. As my orgasm hit, I happily drowned in the depths of swirling pleasure. From a distance I heard my name. Was it angels?

"Karen open on register one, please. Register one."

Damn. My lunch break had come and gone faster than I had.

Sir Christopher slid from my body; the leash loosened; I stood and ran an unsteady hand through my hair.

"You're shaking," he said, turning me and kissing my dampened forehead.

When I still didn't move, Christopher bent down and pulled my jeans up over my legs and hips. We stared at each other, as he zipped and snapped them. The shock of our encounter faded. I couldn't help but grin.

"Tomorrow night?" he asked, unhooking the leash and unbuckling the collar.

I grabbed his hands. "Sure. Want me to wear this again?"

He kissed my mouth, slowly and gently, before saying, "Why don't we explore the produce section?"

I smiled. "Zucchini is on sale. All sizes. Three for a dollar."

His eyebrows rose. "Really? I'll have to see what exotic recipes I can experiment with." He slipped my smock over my sweater that I had retrieved from the floor and tucked my panties into the pocket. We both laughed.

"*Karen!* Where the heck are you?" Herb's voice echoed over the loudspeaker. In the background I heard Cindy. "She said she was going to help some guy with a cleanup on aisle ten."

Christopher pulled me to him, kissing me hard, then setting me aside. I bit my lip and watched him, all lean and cool, as he walked toward the front of the store. Cindy passed him heading toward me, as I stooped to put the scattered merchandise back on the shelf.

“Man, look at that mess. Who was that guy?” she asked, glancing back at the man rounding the aisle to the register.

I shrugged, as I picked up a pink Velcro collar with a tiny bell. I shook it and smiled. “We just met, but I’ll be glad to help him with a cleanup on this aisle anytime.”

MADELINE MOORE

LITTLE BLACK DRESS

LET ME TRY IT ON," said Melissa. The dress was perfect, as if it'd been designed for what she had in mind, but would it fit? It was one of a kind. She was in that sort of shop—the kind with perfect squares of tissue between folds of fabric and pockets closed with a single stitch. Not that the dress had either. It was black suede except for a panel from the waist to the bottom of the bust. That was black leather. The suede was embossed with paisley shapes, black on black, so they could hardly be seen. They provided texture more than a pattern.

The saleswoman suited the store: elegant and skeletal. She led Melissa into a spacious dressing room. There was a chair and magazines, perhaps for indulgent husbands or lovers who'd come along to help pick out an outfit and, more likely than not, to pay for it. But Melissa shopped alone.

It was when she shopped solo that she experienced the deepest, most thrilling rush—the kind that made her cheeks burn and her pulse race and her breathing a little ragged. Like sex? Like the best sex, more like danger or breaking the law—a recklessness that was sometimes worth the price of an exquisite garment she knew she'd never wear. Not this time, though. If this dress fit she'd wear it all right.

If it fit.

Apprehension tinged the air, already redolent with anticipation. The saleswoman uttered a single, encouraging *tsk* and slid the dress from the hanger. Melissa saw that there were squares of tissue, after all, bunched inside each of the slightly puffed short sleeves. The saleswoman tugged out the tissue with her manicured nails. The sleeves, which Melissa had hoped wouldn't be silly, relaxed into sexy little caps that harmonized with the low-cut, sweetheart neckline. Melissa stroked the neckline. There was a weight to the fabric, a heaviness that would be heavenly on. Like a real hide. A moan escaped her mouth. She bit it off, but the saleswoman had heard. She merely nodded; Melissa closed her eyes and gave in to the sensation.

"Nice, yes?" The woman was European, of course. Her dark eyes sparkled. Her barely-there brows arched above them, indicating that the question wasn't meant to be rhetorical, though it very well could have been.

"Exquisite." Melissa kicked off her slides and stripped to her panties. If she'd been alone, she'd have taken them off, too, as she intended to be naked beneath the dress, but since the saleswoman made no motion to leave her alone, she left them on. There'd be no panty line, not with a dress this substantial.

The invisible zipper rasped, then the leather was lowered over her head. The saleswoman started talking about the designer's triumphant show in Paris and how he'd recently selected just three shops in all of North America to carry his merchandise. Melissa half-listened but she was grateful for the background noise. It made the hammering echo of her heartbeat inside her head less overwhelming. She stood with her arms up. It had to fit. For a moment everything went black, then her warm body was welcoming the sheath of cool leather, eager to make the hide live and breathe again.

There was the telling sound of the zipper closing and the leather molding to her hips and breasts.

"Perfect," the saleswoman purred in her ear.

Melissa took a deep breath and tried to relax. The saleswoman plucked at the sleeves and smoothed the dress down from her armpits to her waist. Melissa eyed herself critically. The fit was good, very good. It was low cut, but that was okay, her breasts filled the bodice and spilled, creamy white and smooth and round, not flattened at all by the material, from the neckline. She lifted her arms, and the dress moved with her, no binding, no bunching. She turned this way and that, admiring the fit, the little slit up the back, the way the hem just grazed the tops of her knees. Even in bare feet, with no stockings, the look was decidedly sexy. The fabulous rush of excitement rose again, engulfing her. Her heartbeat was a hard thrum at her temples.

"How much?" she whispered. Not long ago she would have gasped at the reply, but now the more it cost, the better. She had a lot of money. Too much, if some were to be believed. Still, she swooned a little. The little black dress cost far more than she'd ever spent on a piece of clothing.

"But this dress is worth it," murmured the saleswoman.

Melissa turned her back to the mirror and twisted to look over her shoulder. Her face was hot with shameful excitement; she avoided her own eyes. She was helpless, swept away on a sea of want from which she did *not* wish to be rescued.

"You see how it moves with your body? Even though it's suede it isn't cumbersome, is it?"

This time, Melissa didn't answer. She didn't need encouragement. The deal was almost done. Slowly, gracefully, she sank to her knees, watching the mirrors. The suede skirt slid up her thighs. Her bare knees touched the floor. Her ass was a new, curvy line in the shape of the dress. There was a moment of silence.

"I'll take it," she said. She grinned up at the slightly perturbed saleswoman. "It's mine," she murmured, surprising them both.

Acquiring the dress gave her a boost that carried Melissa through the next few days. And then it was party time.

He was being feted by one of his rich, silver-haired, sycophantic bitches and she'd pulled out all the stops, sparing no expense to make his good-bye party the talk of the town. The mansion was decked in silver and white, champagne was flowing, the place was crowded with his fellow diplomats and their entourages. The stage was set.

Melissa slipped into the crowd as unobtrusively as possible, given that she was wearing the dress. Her chestnut hair was swept up in a complicated, messy chignon. She wore a lot of makeup but not too much for such a glitzy event. Black stilettos, of course, and a slim black leather clutch. She carried a silver gift bag. Melissa wore no jewelry whatsoever—her skin was the only accessory she needed with this dress, and vice versa. Did he really think he would ever find, anywhere, skin as soft and pale as hers? As if to prove her point, her throat pulsed blue with every breath. That wasn't it, he'd sworn up and down. "I couldn't ask you to give up everything," he'd said. As if he'd *ever asked* her for anything.

His jaw dropped when he saw her, though her arrival wasn't a surprise. He was caught mid-pontification, his index finger stuck midair. "Melissa!"

She sank to her knees. The dress slithered up her stockinged legs with a hiss.

Gratifyingly, the crowd parted. He stared. She raised her face and stared right back; her ivy-colored eyes misted with tears. Her expression held no challenge. She wasn't here to shame him, or even to shame herself. Her cause was pure. She was sure of it.

He was in front of her now, gesturing with his hands that she should rise. Did he imagine that he could minimize the moment by cutting it short? Jaws had dropped all round. The cat was out of the bag.

"Master?" She was trembling and she knew she'd paled to a ghostly white but she caught his gray glance and held it with hers.

"What do you want?"

"Take me with you, or kill me, please."

There—she'd done it—powered the moment straight past safety into peril. She'd handed him a way out of this mess; he could call her crazy and be done with it all. But would he?

"Come with me." He held out his hand and helped her rise.

It seemed like seconds later they were fucking. He pushed her ahead of him into the first bedroom he could find, then roughly pressed her against the door and devoured her mouth. His hand slid between her breast and the suede bodice of her dress, adding another layer of skin, this one busy and rough. He gripped her breast, hard. She nipped his lower lip and he groaned.

They stumbled farther into the room, clinging to each other. He threw her faceup on the bed. She lay where she landed, not daring to move a muscle. Had she pushed him too far?

He leaned on the bed on one knee and shook the contents of the gift bag out. His hands closed around her throat. "You bitch," he said. "Not too proud, is that it? Not too successful?"

She nodded. "I'm your slave," she whispered. "I belong with you." Her throat fluttered against his hands when she spoke.

He released her. Melissa swallowed. Then his hands were back, this time to buckle the black leather collar, which he'd retrieved from the bedclothes, around her neck. When he was done, she risked a coquettish look. "Pretty?" She shot him a mischievous glance from between lowered lashes.

"Crazy bitch," he said. He rolled her onto her belly and slapped her suede-covered ass soundly. The result was such a satisfying smack he did it a dozen more times before pushing the hem up to her hips.

Melissa struggled to all fours as he dragged her closer to the edge of the bed. They were both panting now. His zipper rasped. His hands fumbled between her legs, long, quick fingers stirring her sex till its juices scalded her thighs. She was ready for him, had been since the last time they'd parted, as she had been that time too, and the time before, and even before that.

He shoved the head of his cock inside her and stirred again, until she moaned. "Please…" she began but he smacked her ass, cutting her off. He thrust hard and all of it slammed up inside her. He gave her six fast, hard strokes before he reached around to finger her clit and the lips that were splayed around his cock.

"You crazy bitch," he said again. She didn't try to answer, just moaned because it was true, all too true. She'd give it all up for him, give up everything she'd acquired so she could be with him—be his slave, his domestic pet. His beast.

He used his fingers and cock to drag her to the precipice, and threw her, screaming, over the edge. Her strangled pleasure sounds made him come, too, as they always did. He roared, oblivious to his surroundings. He fucked her violently, bucking against her. She bucked back, taking him a millimeter deeper, until her cunt was fitted around the entire length of his cock like a sheath. They stayed like that, grinding and moaning until the last spasm trembled to an end.

He collapsed on top of Melissa. She could barely breathe but she didn't care, she didn't dare move or speak. It had been a great fuck but that wasn't nearly all she was after.

He was the first to stir. He puffed out his cheeks and exhaled slowly. It sounded resigned. Her heart made a little, hopeful flip. "Well, come on then, we'd better go make our apologies to our guests," he said.

It didn't take either of them long to tidy up—they'd been undone this way in the past, though not in quite such a spectacular manner. "You need a passport to come home with me," he said. "You have one I assume?"

She nodded. She was afraid to break the spell with words. What if he wasn't serious?

But he was. "After that we'll see about you joining me on my new post." He squinted for a moment, thinking out loud. "It might be easier if we just get married," he muttered.

When he opened the door Melissa hesitated. She looked at him questioningly; her collar was still at her throat.

He shrugged. "Oh, what the hell," he said, "we're leaving town."

Becoming the wife of a diplomat made her job twice as hard, but that was okay. She had plenty of energy. Even motherhood didn't faze Melissa all that much. She knew she was exactly where she belonged.

That was the first and last time Melissa wore her collar in public. The first and last time she wore the dress, too. But she cherished both of them forever.

Every so often, when Melissa thought about what she'd done that day, she was overwhelmed with something close to horror. A frigid shiver of disbelief rippled down her backbone. How had she ever found the nerve to go there, alone, and kneel before him and all his bon voyage guests? How had she *dared*?

At such times she'd hurry to the master bedroom and push her way to the back of the walk-in closet. She kept the dress behind her huge, plastic-sheathed, white satin wedding gown, hidden in its great shadow. She'd fall upon it, clutching it as gently as possible while she breathed in its animal smell. Melissa's heartbeat would pound in her ears, but it was a steady, solid sound. She *had* dared. And she'd never been entirely alone. She'd been wearing her little black dress.

SHANE ALLISON

DANGEROUS COMFORT

LUCKILY, I've never been so much as five minutes late to a movie. Hell, it's better to be an hour or two early I always say. Tonight I was tickled fucking pink I didn't have to stand in some long-ass line. I came around the corner to find that both box offices had lines that formed along Garfield's Bar and Grill, and damn near out of the double glass doors of the mall. I jetted past couples, teenagers and families of screaming babies, straight up to the boy tearing tickets. I had found an admissions ticket in my wallet folded between my tattered voter's registration card and two unpaid carbon-copy traffic citations that were so kindly given to me by Tallahassee's finest for running a red light and making an illegal U-turn. *Need to pay these fuckin' things*, I thought as I fished out my untorn ticket for *Constantine*.

"First theater to your left," he said. This was one of the smaller theaters with pathetic sound and hard seats. Not like the bigger theaters with THX sound and enough foot room to spread a sleeping bag in.

"Is this the only theater this movie's showing in?" I asked.

"Yeah, sorry," he replied. I walked in to check if I needed to get a seat right away or if I had enough time to get something to eat. The place was sparse, but filling up fast. I had ten minutes to spare before the coming attractions. There were four people ahead of me: a heavy, big duke of a dude who looked as if he was ordering everything off the menu that hung above the refreshment stand. From popcorn to jumbo pretzels, this man's hands were full of movie food. The skater boy in front of him with ratty, bleached-blond dreads was growing impatient, and so was I. The previews are the best part. I looked at my watch to find that I had five minutes left. Fat-ass stuffed his change in his plus-size pants, grabbed his feast off the counter and started down the lobby.

Finally, damn, I thought. Skater boy was up next. He ordered a strawberry slushee and a box of Jujyfruits, which I hate. I'm more of a Raisinette man myself. There were two young honeys going on about who's the finest, Usher or Ray J. Up in here looking like something right out of *King* magazine. Fine as hell too. They bought a box of Sour Patch Kids and switched them fine asses around the corner to their respective theater.

Before the concession operator could ask if she could help me, I blurted out, "Small popcorn, no butter!" I gave her four bucks and told her to keep the change. When I walked in, there were only a few seats left. Some people were holding spots for friends while you had evil bitches who would sit their pocketbooks in the seats next to them to keep people like me from asking if they were taken. I thought, *What is this, a movie theater or a school bus?* I didn't want to sit in the back only to be bothered by patrons still trying to squeeze into an already packed movie. Didn't want to end my ass up in the front and risk suffering whiplash and burning eyes from sitting too close. I was going to wait until the next showing when I noticed a few empty seats in the middle row.

There were these two dudes sitting in the first two seats near the aisle. I think they were punks 'cause they were sitting way too close to be "boyz." "Are those seats down there taken?" I said. I never thought I would be asking that shit. Not me, Mr. Johnny Come Fuckin' Early.

"No," they said. I stepped over them saying excuse and pardon me. I took the last seat next to the wall. I hadn't yet made myself comfortable enough before the lights started to dim. Theater patrons were steadily rolling in, making their way down the aisle. As I munched on salty popcorn, this couple was standing at the edge of the row that the gay dudes and I shared. It was continuing to fill up except for two empty seats down by where I was sitting. I looked over and watched the shorty whisper something to one of them sitting on the end. I don't much like people I don't know sitting next to me. I usually have a female on my arm, but I decided to take a break from the shorties tonight. This female was fine though. It was so dark; I couldn't really see how she looked face-wise except for the thick mane of weave that draped along her back.

I staked my claim by securing my spot on the armrest. As they grew closer to my end of the row, she started to come in clearer. She was a brown-skin honey wearing a leather jacket stretched over a set of titties that were nice I'm sure. She had on one of them leather skirts that was hugging her junk tight. I didn't much care about her man. I was too busy watching this leather-clad honey dip. She sat her fine self next to me. The scent of leather was strong, mixing in with popcorn. I moved in closer to her to take a whiff of what that jacket was giving off. Just to smell it made me feel fifty feet tall. The texture of the leather glowed in the glare from the Fanta commercial.

I sat the salty popcorn on the floor next to my feet and wiped my fingers on my jeans as the movie started. She began peeling off her jacket to get more comfortable. She worked them cute arms one at a time out of leathered sleeves. The intoxicating aroma filled my lungs.

Yep, I thought. *Nice tits.*

When she leaned over in my direction and whispered, "Would you mind at all if I lay this 'cross our laps?" I swear to God, I got a hard-on right then and there. The girl spoke country, a Georgia gal, a sweet peach right here in the sunshine state. Her breath was like watermelon bubble gum as she whispered them words in my ears I inherited from Granddaddy.

"No problem."

"Thank you," she said. "I just don't want to get it messed up."

Her jacket covered us like an electric blanket. The heat beneath us was beginning to circle with my twitching dick misbehaving in the cotton tomb of my underwear. People were starting to simmer and settle with nothing but the sound of popcorn being crunched on, and sodas being slurped. Things were quiet with just the sound of Keanu Reeves kicking demon ass in wide-screen mayhem. As the movie went on, the soft arm of this hot, black-haired beauty started grazing up against me. She pulled away each time she felt skin on skin, but a split second later her knee touched mine. I watched her from the corner of my eye not knowing whether these moves she was making were accidental or intentional. Even though I'm adamant about the armrest, I made an exception for her and moved over slightly, allowing her a bit of room to rest her arm, keep her from having to lull such a pretty limb in her lap. I watched her closely. She took in what I have to offer.

My palms started to sweat as the heat from the leather swirled beneath in our laps. The flesh of my elbow kissed the flesh of hers. She moved her arm steady away; I veered in with a knee against her knee. She slid one of them long legs across the floor sticky with soda. This lady was hard to get, but I always get what I want. I'd missed the whole plot of the movie because of her, but who cared? I'd catch it again at Cinema Twin where the seats literally come loose from the floor, where you're lucky to catch the ending before the projectors falter.

I pulled one hand from beneath her jacket that smelled of perfume, and set it on the black hide. I only had my left hand now, using my pinkie finger to caress mahogany skin. I was scared as hell she'd turn and yell rape, break my bones with barbwire words. She smelled like angels oughta smell: the perfect woman, soft under the lap of leather. I moved with a steady pace across the bridge of her arm, careful not to bring attention to her man sitting next to her. One wrong move, if the jacket slipped, there'd be a reckoning. I moved my hand between her legs, gliding it up silken thighs. I watched her nervously, examining her reaction. Nothing except for the one going on in my jeans. This had never happened to me before. Not with any female. Her middle grew hotter to the touch as I stirred under the leather tent of her skirt, getting closer to her cunt.

I moved my right hand under the jacket to work my dick. The belt around my waist wasn't tight and I slid my hand past the waistband of my underwear, over rough pubic hair. My dick was stiff and sweaty. My other hand struggled with her stockings, tore easily through them to get to her, hoping that no one heard the rip but me and this angel. I pulled back panties and I was in. She was wet as fuck down there. Sloppy and Southern. The leather's scent steeped with sweat and perfume, making a toxic, musky mixture that worked itself through our skin, through a lightening bolt of veins, a flood of hot blood.

My hand was caught in her web of silk and nylon. Fingers skimmed along supple pussy lips and a tough dick in a simultaneous dance of masturbation with only the black jacket to hide my nasty act. I glanced peripherally into her blouse. The glare from the screen bounced off her sugar-brown breasts. I wanted to reach down into the satin of sleeves and seams and cop a feel, my tongue exploring dark nipples. I noticed her hand on the left of her bracing the armrest as I pushed deep within her cunt. Pearls of sweat trickled along my face and down my chin as I moved my two middle fingers in and out again. As I fingered her through, I steady jacked off under her jacket, thinking of this dick in her stuff. It didn't take me long to come. I burned and tensed in my britches.

I could feel semen coming as Keanu went head to head with the devil dressed to the teeth in a white suit. I wiped my hand on my jeans as I fingered her slow, careful to remember that I was in a public place and not the El Camino Motel with some stripper. I liked the feeling of her lips constricting around my fingers like her pussy had a mind of its own. I watched her with peripheral vision; saw her shut her eyes, each muscle in her Nubian face tensing, that hand of hers bracing her armrest as I fucked her steady with these fingers. She was about ready to pop and I didn't stop till she came. Felt like she was having twenty orgasms down there. Good pussy.

I eased to a crawl, finishing her off. I slid my fingers out of her spent cunt, from beneath her leather skirt, gliding her sweet scent under my nose. My fingers coasted along my lips, slipping into my mouth for a taste. I stared down at her as she adjusted herself beneath the leather. The movie ended. Good kicked evil's ass again. The credits rolled, the lights came up and people started to file out of the sardine-sized theater.

Without so much as a glance back at me, she stood and followed her man out the row, the two of them descending hand in hand down carpeted steps.

"That was good," I heard him say.

Sho' was, I said to myself. What we did was better than any Hollywood blockbuster.

MICHELLE HOUSTON

TEMPTED

LEAVING OUT THE FACT that I am not a fan of the whole "meat market" that nightclubs have become, I have to admit the views are sometimes great. A good example would be the tight ass in leather pants shimmying out on the dance floor, about five steps away from where I was sitting. My nipples tightened and my pussy clenched just looking at her. Damn good view. Whatever it is about women in leather that turns me on, I really don't care. So long as women keep wearing it, I'll be happy.

Then again, I've never been one to overanalyze much of anything that has to do with sex. All those years of psych classes kind of made me afraid to get too deep into my own head. So now, I settle for getting paid to delve into the deep, dark places within the minds of others.

Speaking of deep, dark places! Her front view was as good as the back. Second on my list of things I like, after leather, would have to be midriff shirts and belly rings. If only I hadn't been about twenty years her senior, she'd have been perfect for me. Until she opened her mouth.

"Professor?"

Shit!

"I'm sorry, do I know you?"

"Professor Marcum. I'm Brittany. I had you for Psych 101 last semester."

"Brittany? Oh yes, you sat up front with Ariel and Svetlana."

"So you do remember me."

I wasn't sure how she did it, but even as she was talking, and without my noticing it, she had pulled out a chair right next to me and straddled it. "I never would have dreamed of running into you here."

Maybe it was visions of my entire career flushing down the drain that had kept me from noticing her sitting down. Because if she told anyone at the school, I could be fired from my teaching position. Although I enjoy helping my clients, teaching had become the new direction I wanted my life to take. She seemed to understand immediately.

"I'll make you a deal, Professor."

I arched an eyebrow at her, trying to mold my face into my stern look, knowing it failed miserably. Three margaritas tended to make me mellow. Since this was my career on the line, I would have thought my body would be a bit more cooperative. Knowing I wasn't going to be able to stare her down, I settled for waiting to hear her ultimatum. She had earned an *A* in my class.

"Dance with me, and I won't tell a soul that I saw you here tonight or any other night you care to come back."

Of all the things she could have asked for, she wanted to dance?

"Dance with me, and I'll keep your secret. You're in a club after all, and I haven't seen you dance since you came in, not once."

I latched on to the only excuse I had. "I can't dance."

I really didn't want to go out on the dance floor with her, but not for that reason. I was quite simply afraid of letting her know how much she affected me.

Even with her sitting there, I was horny. I'm not sure what perfume she was wearing, but it made my head spin. And if the shirt she was wearing dipped any lower, I was going to see her belly button from the top.

"That's okay, I'll teach you."

Before I had a chance to offer another excuse, she clasped my hand in hers and stood, pulling me with her. Unlike my own, rough from years of gardening, hers was silky smooth. I couldn't help but wonder if the rest of her was so tanned and smooth and utterly kissable beneath her leather pants and slinky top.

I trembled just thinking about it. Luckily, she didn't seem to notice as we were already weeding our way through the crowd to the far edge of the dance floor, where there were less people.

"Just listen to the beat of the music and let it flow through you, not to you. Leave the rest to me." Before I knew what she was about she had plastered herself against me, her hands holding my hips tightly as she slid a leg between mine.

"Miss Collins—"

"It's Brittany, Elaine. I'm not your student anymore, and you're no longer my teacher. Now, *I'm* the teacher"—at that she giggled slightly—"and you have to relax and trust me."

She shifted against me, driving her leather-clad leg against my crotch. I bit back a moan as she slid it again, the friction delicious to my sex-starved pussy. Her hips started moving in circles against mine, while her hands guided me into the rhythm. Soon I was lost within the beat and the heat of her embrace, wishing things best left unwished. It had been so long since I'd allowed anyone this close to me, and my body was awake, demanding I satisfy its needs.

Brittany pressed her face into the curve of my neck, and I wanted nothing more than to pull her closer and kiss her, while sliding my hands through the dark curls on her head.

It took a moment for the light flicks against my neck to register as kisses, but when they did, I reared back in shock. "Brittany, what are you—" Then she kissed me, full on the mouth. In that moment of weakness, I parted my lips and kissed her back.

It was utterly incredible. I fisted my hands in her hair, as I'd imagined, holding her against me while I allowed her to ravage my mouth. Her groin shifted against mine, and all I wanted to do was lay her down and bury my face between her legs.

"We can't be doing this," I managed to protest.

"Why not? I like you, and I'm guessing you like me, too." As her hand cupped my crotch, I nearly jumped to the ceiling. The thin layers of linen and silk that separated her hand from the very heat of my body didn't seem all that thick. "No one is paying the slightest bit of attention to us."

Guiltily, I looked around, waiting for someone to make eye contact, but all around me women were lost in the movements of the dance, molding themselves to their partners, so that in the dim light of the dance floor you couldn't be certain where one ended and the other began.

Her hand slid up a bit, her fingers brushing against my stomach as she gently slid them past the waistband of my slacks, down between my panties and skin. "Touch me," she whispered, as tempting as the sirens of myth. My hands twitched at my sides as she brushed my clit with her fingertip.

Leaning in, I kissed her, my tongue sweeping past her parted lips to mate with hers. One of my hands settled on her hip, drawing her tight against me. Two of her long, slender fingers slid past my pussy lips, even as I was cupping her crotch in my other hand.

The feel of leather under my fingertips was exquisite. I couldn't help but remember my last lover, who had delighted in wearing a black leather harness to hold her dildo in place while she fucked me from behind. The black always contrasted so nicely with her sweet complexion that just seeing her wear it was enough to make me cream. But that was so long ago, and Brittany was my here and now. For just this brief interlude, with her leather pants and her brash, take-charge attitude, she was mine. Yet like a wild thing, she wasn't mine to keep, I knew.

As her fingers slid deeper inside me, I moaned into her mouth. She kissed me harder, consuming my inhibitions and my will, until I was nothing but a bundle of nerves, craving her touch.

I slid my hand from her hip and cupped her leather-clad ass, as I gently unzipped her pants and slid the other hand against the welcoming heat of her core, where I made the startling discovery that the leather was moist with her essence, because she wasn't wearing anything beneath it. I almost fainted.

“Yes,” she breathed against my lips. “Finger me, right here on the floor.”

The thrill alone was enough to make my pulse race. Here I was, in a lesbian bar, with a former student whose hand was down my pants, while I was intimately touching her. Tracing the slick line of her pussy lips, I gently parted them and thrust my middle finger deep. Brittany laid her head against my shoulder. She moaned softly in my hair, as I continued to manipulate her pussy in time to her touches against mine.

Although I'd always been able to get off on penetration, I had never been as revved up as I was now. As she thrust her fingers in and out, driving me slowly out of my mind, I wanted to rip off my clothes and sink to the floor. Just once wasn't going to be enough—but I knew I was greedy to ever think of asking her for more.

So I gave myself up to the moment, and her touch, and the feel of her juices coating my hand. Gently, I rubbed the pad of my thumb against her clit, manipulating the tiny bundle of nerves as much as I could within the tight confines.

Brittany continued to thrust her fingers into me, until without much warning I climaxed, right there on the dance floor. The analytical part of my mind was shocked that I was allowing it to happen in such a public way, where anyone could see. And with a former student no less, someone I only knew within the context of a classroom setting. But it was also an incredible rush, and utterly forbidden. Dizzy, I continued to sway against her, the sweet friction of her movements prolonging my euphoria.

As my heartbeat started to return to normal, I doubled my efforts on her clit, with great reward. Her teeth nipped at my neck as she convulsed in my arms. Faintly, I could hear Brittany's moans as her juices trickled into my hand. The smell of wet leather teased my senses and I wrapped my free arm around her waist, holding her close as she came.

All around us, people danced on. I'm sure some had to know what we were doing, but no one seemed to care. They were as lost in each other as Brittany and I were in creating a moment to remember.

As tenderly as I could, I extracted my hands from her pants and zipped her back up. Lifting my fingertips to my lips, I licked them clean, savoring the heady mixture of her juices and the smell of damp leather. I wanted to drop to my knees, bury my face into her groin, and inhale deeply.

"Brittany I—"

"Shhh," she cut me off, pressing a finger to my lips. Without conscious thought, I sucked it into my mouth, tasting myself for the first time in a long time.

"No promises, no regrets. Take a week to think things over. I'll be here next Saturday, same time."

Reaching up I clasped her hand in mine and pulled it away from my lips. Pressing a soft kiss to her lips, I whispered, "Wear leather for me." Then I allowed her to walk away. As she moved across the bar, I watched her tight ass swaying, cupped so intimately by her leather pants.

MIKE KIMERA

OTHER BONDS THAN LEATHER

LOOK, WOULD I HAVE TO CALL YOU MASTER?" Caroline says, doing an Igor impersonation as she twists the word. "Because I don't think I could do that without giggling."

"Not if you don't want to."

"But I thought the whole point of this dom/sub thing was to make me do things I don't want to do."

"The point is to make you do things you deeply desire and don't dare to do."

"What kind of things?" She's still smiling, but with a real question in her eyes.

"That's what we we'd find out together, Caroline. Isn't that why you are here?"

"I'm here—against my better judgment if truth be known—because something about you tugs at me. I think it's your voice. I'm perfectly sane until I hear your voice and then suddenly I find myself wanting…"

"Wanting what?"

"I don't know." She laughs again, nervously this time. "For you to like me? To give me your approval?" Her voice lowers. "To invite me into your world?"

"So being here with me isn't sane?"

"Well, look at me," she says, holding out her arms. "What do you see? An older, heavier woman with big thighs and small breasts who ought to know better. I mean, I'm going to be a grandmother soon."

Now it's my turn to laugh. I take her right hand and hold it in both of mine. I pull her closer and say, "What I see is a woman who intrigues me. An intelligent, articulate woman whose sensuality and strength show in everything she does." I kiss her hand. "I see a woman who honored my request not to wear underwear…" (she actually blushes at this) "…and whose thighs invite me to explore."

"That's exactly what I mean," she says, pretending to be cross and pulling her hand away. "Words like that, spoken like that… How am I supposed to make sensible decisions when you drip words like that into my mind?"

"Listen to your lust, Caroline. It'll tell you what to do."

Suddenly she looks serious. "Promise you won't just play with me, Jonathan. Don't make me into a fool."

I match her tone, looking straight into her eyes. "I want you to trust yourself. I want you to trust me. Let go. I promise I will catch you."

I can't read her expression as she rifles my face for signs of betrayal or insincerity. She looks away and asks brightly, "So do you have a dungeon, O Masterly One?"

"Yes," I say.

She raises an eyebrow, whether in disbelief or disapproval I can't tell.

"Follow me, please," I say. I don't look back—but I'm pleased when I hear her on the stairs behind me.

"Holy Penguins, Batman! It's the Bat Cave." Caroline slaps one fist into her palm in a very believable impersonation of Robin.

I stay by the stairs, switching on the spotlights one by one.

She moves around the room slowly, as if she's memorizing an exhibition at the museum.

She starts at the leather Cross of St. Andrew with its restraints at the four extremes of the *X*. Then she circles the stocks, adjusted to just the height for her head and hands. Next the leather hurdle, which she bends over playfully, looking back at me for comment. I switch on the next light.

"Good God." She stares at the whips and collars and paddles hanging on the wall. "Fuck Toys R Us." Her eyes fall on the bench displaying dildos, butt plugs, restraints and gags. She's like a sleepwalker now: her movements slow and her eyes everywhere at once. She picks up an inflatable penis gag, and then drops it as if it were hot after she sees what happens when she squeezes the bladder. Her fingers move gently over the black silicone of the largest butt plug. When she turns to me, her nipples are erect under her summer dress, but her eyes are in shock.

"You...use all these?"

"Usually not all at the same time," I say.

"Women let you tie them up and put these things on them—in them—and..." She's speaking slowly. The reality of "my world," the world she wanted to be invited into, is hitting her for the first time.

"Would you like to leave, Caroline? Shall I take you back upstairs? We can have a glass of wine before you go home?"

She shakes her head.

I switch on one more light and then switch off the rest.

In the center of the circle of warm bright light is a gyniechair, complete with stirrups. It has straps at the wrists and neck.

Caroline stares. She has her back to me and is moving away from the chair as if she's not aware she's doing it.

I turn her gently by the shoulders until she's facing me.

"Close your eyes please, Caroline." My voice is calm, reasonable, compelling.

A small hesitation, a tremor of doubt, and then her eyes close.

I have to bend to kiss her. I hold her face in my hands, my thumbs gently tracing her cheekbones. My lips press hers—but it is her tongue that enters my mouth. She's eager now. Her arms wrap around me; her whole body is trying to adhere to mine. My left hand is stroking her hair. Short, wiry, strong, sexy; her hair is a metaphor for the woman herself. The tension in her body passes slowly from anxiety to desire. I break the kiss but do not release her head from my hands.

"I want you to sit in the chair with your legs in the stirrups." I let go and her head turns toward the chair.

"I want to explore the space between your thighs," I say, leading her toward the circle of light.

She stops at the chair. We are in the struggle now, she and I; the dance has begun. I can feel her unspoken words pushing at me.

"I won't tie you or gag you or blindfold you today, but I want you to do what I ask. If you decide not to, we will go back upstairs." I might lose her here.

A fire of anger that stirs my cock flashes through her eyes, but she suppresses it.

"If you hurt me, I'll leave," she says.

Touché. This is going to be interesting.

Caroline looks small in the chair. Without being told, she lifts her dress so that her sex is fully exposed. She has trimmed her pubic hair, but a defiant banner of gray-streaked curls covers her mons.

I stand between her brightly lit legs and look intently at her sex. She squirms a little; uncomfortable at being so exposed.

"You look magnificent," I say. Then, before she can reply, I say, "Please close your eyes and keep them closed. Keep your hands on the arms of the chair."

She closes her eyes.

I count to ten. I know it will seem longer to her. She doesn't speak. I smile: the dance has progressed.

I run my index fingers down the inside of her thighs. The skin is soft, getting softer as I reach the top. I stop just where the thigh joins the hip, both fingers on either side of her cunt but not touching it. Then I let go.

Her eyes are still closed. Good.

I unzip. Slowly. The sound is loud in the silence of the room.

My index fingers repeat their journey but this time lightly touching the outer labia.

I pull a condom from my pocket. I hold it close to Caroline so she'll hear the packet being ripped open and smell the latex. Then I lay it on the palm of her right hand like a promise. Her hand opens and closes on it; she says nothing.

On their third journey along her thighs my index fingers spread the plump outer labia wide. They don't retreat this time but hold her open; she glistens like an oyster in the spotlight.

"Oh, God. Do it. Fuck me," Caroline says.

I ignore her and kneel between her thighs. Her clit is small but unsheathed now. I move the flesh around it with my fingers but leave it untouched. Then I turn my head and push my tongue as deep into her as I can. She coats my tongue and my cock throbs.

Still inside her, I turn the tip of my tongue upward and try to scoop out her juices.

"Fuck, yes," Caroline says.

I remove my tongue. It aches a little but it tastes wonderful.

I stand.

"Keep your eyes closed but give me the condom please, Caroline."

If she keeps the condom the dance will end.

She opens her hand for me.

When she feels the rubber slide into her cunt she gasps. Her face telegraphs her concern. Despite her words earlier, she's still not sure if she really wants to fuck. This is happening too quickly.

A second or two later she realizes the condom is stretched over three of my fingers. Her laugh turns to a moan as the fingers find her G-spot.

When my tongue flicks across her clit she literally bounces in the stirrups. Her come starts when I suck her clit into my mouth and hold it.

I knew she'd be loud. The sound and taste of her make me dizzy.

I withdraw my fingers and remove the condom.

She is still breathing hard when I move to stand behind her chair.

"What a wet cunt you have," I whisper. "What a sweet-tasting slit."

Then, bending forward, I push my juice-coated tongue into her mouth. She sucks. Hard.

When the kiss stops she says, "Thank you," almost as if she were talking in her sleep.

"Open your eyes, Caroline."

She blinks at the bright light as I remove her legs from the stirrups and help her down from the chair. She leans into me and her hand goes to my erection. "May I?" she says, moving her hand along the shaft.

"Next time, perhaps," I say and move her hand away.

"Why not?" she says in a tone that gives me a flashback of her as she must have been as a little girl, stamping her foot to get her way.

I push my cock back inside my jeans. "Because I want my first come to be inside you when you're bound to that cross." I point at the *X*-frame across the room.

She steps away from me.

"Is that a power play, Jonathan?" she says.

"No, it's a fantasy. I want you completely open to me. I want to feel you give your whole body to me. When you are ready."

"You are a strange man," she says.

"Yes," I reply.

Mimicking my earlier action, she lifts my hand and kisses it. "Thank you, Jonathan. I enjoyed today. But I need time to think."

I put my arm around her and lead her back to the real world.

After she leaves, I go back to the playroom, strip and sit in the chair. I can still feel her presence. She has promised to come back, tomorrow, when she has had time to think.

I close my eyes and work my cock slowly.

I summon her taste and smell. I imagine her asking to be tied to my cross. I concentrate on the image of her being pummeled into the leather and groaning with pleasure.

Caroline believes there was no bondage today. No restraints were used. She does not yet know that there are other bonds than leather, that all restraint is a matter of will.

As my spend slides over my hand and onto my belly, I think that my new bonds feel good. I shall wear them yet awhile.

LISETTE ASHTON

TRUMAN CAPOTE WAS WRONG

LINDA PULLED THE MATRIX COAT tight across her chest as she hurried through the city. It was a glossy black vinyl, pungent and fashioned to resemble the garment worn by the character Trinity in *Matrix Reloaded* and *Matrix Revolution*. The tailored fit stretched tight across her hips and breasts when fastened. But on days like this—when she was hurrying with the buttons undone and the weather was against her—the tails billowed in her wake as though she wore a cape.

Slate skies, as drab as the smog-stained skyscrapers, broiled overhead. She trotted briskly through the streets, leaving the bustle of traffic and pedestrians behind as she headed toward narrow lanes and the city's forgotten corners. The wide roads became claustrophobic alleyways. The grimy pavement turned to litter-strewn cobbles. The faraway toll of Big Ben declared she was already late but, hoping against hope that she could make her appointment, Linda hurried on.

Her chest heaved from the exertion. Her muscles ached. Panic rose at the back of her throat as she feared seeing the CLOSED sign. Not allowing herself to dwell on that image, sure it would come true if she visualized it, Linda rounded a corner and hurried on toward the wrought-iron railings that surrounded the shop's modest forecourt.

Cream blinds were drawn behind the plate glass windows.

She glanced at the wooden door, ignoring the peeling paint blistering away from its surface. Her gaze was fixed on the cataclysmic sign in the door's window: CLOSED.

"Shit!"

In the silence of the empty street she could hear her lungs wheezing for breath. Her heartbeat raced and pounded after the effort of hurrying to the tailor's. Big Ben had stopped chiming and the sounds of the city were as far away as her chances of collecting her order. After the noise of her race to make the appointment the silence was a proclamation of her defeat.

"Shit! Shit! Shit!"

"Linda?"

She flinched, startled by the tailor's voice.

The dapper little man—his three-piece suit a testament to his skills for style, craftsmanship and fashion—stood by her side. Sparkling eyes studied her from behind wire-rimmed spectacles. "I'd just about given up on you," he confessed.

She considered telling him about her struggle to get out of the office, the cancellation of the Bakerloo line and her frantic dash to take three different tubes to transport her on a circuitous route to the Elephant and Castle junction. She thought of mentioning the overcrowded underground, and the hubbub of noisy indolents who had caused her delay with their slow shuffle through entrances and exits. She even thought of mentioning the arrogant university student who had been quoting Capote at a girl, telling her the writer had said, "*The good thing about masturbation is that you don't have to dress up to do it.*"

Because she knew such an exchange of trivialities would make her time with the tailor mundane, Linda only said, "I'd just about given up on me too."

He chuckled, placed an avuncular hand on her arm, and guided her toward the shop doorway.

Every time Linda had a wet dream she knew her subconscious always used the tailor's shop as a backdrop for the experience. Hearing the discordant jangle of the bell over the door, seeing the familiar swatches of fabric that adorned the shelves and walls, was tantamount to a Pavlovian trigger for her libido. She drew a deep breath and immediately caught the intermingled scents of leather, vinyl, latex, cloth and PVC.

It was a heady blend.

Her heart had been racing from the hasty rush to make her appointment. Now it pounded with the surge of arousal and adrenaline. Her body was jolted by a heightened sense of awareness and she felt inordinately attuned to every nuance in her surrounding atmosphere. Although the tailor had disappeared into a back room she could hear the shuffle of his footsteps as he retrieved her order. In the timeworn rolls of fabric and cloth she could sense the ages each length had remained in waiting. And when the first spatters of rain thudded against the hidden window, she shivered in empathy with the oncoming wetness.

Her own wetness was starting with equal haste.

The room was shaded by the blind.

As the rain began to fall it grew darker.

Grimly, Linda realized the light was hatefully similar to the haze she enjoyed during her most intense fantasies. Those excursions into fantasy began in badly lit gloom until they were finally concluded in an explosion of light so bright it stung her retinas. Unable to stop herself, she trembled. The arousal was already in her lungs, born from a blossom of leather fragrances and vinyl perfumes. The scent was more intoxicating than the strongest amyl nitrate.

"You've graduated to *Underworld*," the tailor chuckled as he returned. "Are you no longer having your love affair with *The Matrix*?"

He was the only person she knew who could pinpoint her likes and dislikes in such succinct terms. She didn't need to argue that the film had struck her as pretentious and incomprehensible. To Linda it had never been more than a fashion catalogue on DVD. "I never had a love affair with *The Matrix*," she said quietly. "I simply liked Trinity's coat in those movies."

"You have an eye for style."

"I fell in love with Selene's outfit when I watched *Underworld*. I think her coat is similar to Trinity's, except Trinity's is vinyl and Selene's is cut from..."

"...Aniline-dyed leather." The tailor finished the sentence for her as he presented her order. He held a massive length of black leather over his arms. The day's fading light glistened against its liquid sheen. The inflections of the patina gave an impression that the hide was alive and moving of its own volition. Linda stared at the coat, mesmerized by the beauty of her latest possession. Reverentially, she drew a soft breath. It took willpower not to snatch the coat from his hands and embrace and caress the glossy black folds.

"It's ready for the final fitting," he told her.

For an instant she couldn't move.

As much as she strove to look cool and ruthless the acquisition of desired beauty always made her hesitate. Doubts—nagging worries that she wasn't worthy to own something so magnificent—plagued her thoughts. She took a moment's reflection to calm her excitement and swallowed the electric taste of spittle from the back of her throat. The smell of the coat was so strong her saliva was flavored with the distinctive taste of leather. The fluid heat between her legs grew wet enough to make its presence known. Eagerly, she shrugged the vinyl from her shoulders and reached out for her new coat.

The tailor took a step back and shook his head.

Her disappointment was strong enough to sting like a cane across bare knuckles. She glared at him with hurt and outrage.

"I want to fit this properly," he explained. "I've invested a lot of time and effort in this creation." His gaze flitted to her blouse and her dark pinstriped pants. "I don't intend this final fitting to be encumbered by *off-the-peg* garments." He emphasized the words with obvious disdain. He studied her from behind his spectacles with quiet anticipation.

Linda could feel color rising in her cheeks. But her blushes weren't roused with the shame of what he was suggesting. She felt more upset that her work clothes had earned the tailor's distaste. Hurriedly she began to pluck the buttons on her blouse.

"Slowly," the tailor assured her. "We have as long as is necessary."

She acted as though she hadn't heard. The blouse came off in a flurry of white nylon and she dropped it to the floor. Standing in her bra and trousers did not cause any upset. They were alone, the shop door was locked and the blind was drawn. He had seen more when he measured her for the Trinity coat. Slipping the trousers from her hips, kicking off her shoes as she freed her legs, Linda stood up to present herself to him in plain white pants and a matching bra. She tossed him a questioning glance.

The tailor shook his head again. "Shouldn't we do this fitting properly?" Behind his wire-rimmed spectacles his eyes shone with mischievous glee.

Linda nodded. She unhooked the bra and allowed it to spill from her breasts. Before the tailor had a chance to see her bare chest she was bending down and removing her pants. She could see a wet stain in the center of the gusset. At the same moment she caught the scent of her musk—strong and feminine. In an instant of astounding clarity she realized the scents of her sex and the fragrance of the new leather were almost identical. The two perfumes were a perfect complement to each other.

"That's more like it," the tailor smiled. He studied her with a gaze that was appreciative and unsolicited but not unpleasant. He stepped closer and offered her the coat.

Linda hesitated before accepting. Her fingers hovered over the smooth jet skin. She remembered reading that there was a technique for caressing lovers where no contact was made with the flesh. The fingers moved less than a millimeter above the surface of a partner, teasing the microscopic hairs that covered every body, warming the skin with the suggestion of their nearness. It wasn't something she had ever tried but she felt as though she was enjoying that sort of experience with this latest acquisition.

"I can't tell you how much pleasure it gives me to see someone who appreciates quality tailoring."

She glanced at the tailor and saw he was admiring the thrust of her rigid nipples. She hadn't realized the symptoms of her arousal were so obvious. Her areolae were stained to the color of flushing rosebuds. She idly wondered if the tailor had caught the fetid scent of her sex, and then decided she didn't care. Whatever pleasure he got from seeing her naked body was equally repaid by the satisfaction she got from wearing his creations.

Knowing it was time for her to take the coat, she lifted it from his arms.

Another shiver went through her.

The leather was as warm as living flesh.

As her fingers made contact with its malleable surface she knew the coat would be the fulfillment of every fantasy she had ever harbored. Savoring the moment, not allowing any distraction to intrude, she brought the collar to her nostrils and inhaled the sultry and distinctive perfume. There was no way to describe the scent because nothing else in the world smelled like leather. The closest thing that came to mind was the feral fragrance of animal passions. The musk from her wet and needy pussy was vaguely reminiscent. But even that inimitable bouquet was not as evocative as the hide she held.

Her pulse quickened. Her nipples ached to be caressed. The inner muscles of her cunt clenched with fresh spasms of hunger. The wetness of her arousal threatened to spill from the lips her sex.

The tailor plucked the coat from her grasp.

For an instant she wanted to snatch it back from him and fight him for ownership. It was only when she realized he was helping her into the garment that she relented and allowed him to hold the shoulders. He stood behind her, and she knew he had an unfettered view of her bare back and buttocks, but that consideration was so immaterial it barely registered on her thoughts. When he lifted the sleeves along her arms, allowing the satin lining to caress the sensitive flesh of her inner wrists, she trembled with mounting excitement.

"You'll need to put your shoes back on," the tailor said quietly. "The length allows for you wearing a three-inch heel. Anything higher and the coat will look out of proportion. Anything lower and the hem will drag on the floor."

She nodded and stepped into the shoes.

The lapels were already caressing her breasts. The satin lining brushed against her buttocks and then smoothed along her thighs. Inside the sleeves her arms were engulfed by the leather. She listened to it creak and mumble wordless enjoyment as it fitted itself to the curves and crevices of her body.

"Comfortable?"

She couldn't speak.

Sensation overload had her teetering on the brink of an experience she hadn't expected. The Trinity coat had made her feel sexual. The vinyl had inspired sufficient orgasms to make the garment a treasured favorite. When she was home, alone and dressed to play, the tight restrictions of the Trinity coat had bound her breasts and hips in a suffocating embrace.

But this was something more.

This was almost spiritual.

"Allow me to fasten it," the tailor said kindly.

She couldn't bring herself to answer. Her heart was racing. She was swathed in long luxuriant leather and reveling in the experience. His fingers went to her throat and fastened the topmost button. She wondered if she might be shaking or if the tailor's hands were trembling with empathy to her arousal. He seemed to caress the sensitive flesh of her neck before managing his chore. His fingers, as smooth and dry as the fabric she now wore, softly stroked beneath her jawline.

The neck fitted so snugly Linda thought it was like the most subversive form of bondage. As he fastened the second and then the third buttons her breasts were bound tight within the coat's confines. Her nipples were crushed against the satin lining and she could see their bulge straining at the smooth patina of the leather's finish. If she had been alone the sight would have made her moan with desire. Because the tailor continued to force buttons through the tight holes she could only remain poised, contain her arousal, and allow him to carry on.

The fourth, fifth and sixth buttons pulled the coat around her waist and hips. The leather had become a second skin, embracing her contours and emphasizing the perfection of her figure. The little man knelt before her as he fastened the final button, his fumbling fingers touching the bare flesh of her inner thighs and grazing lightly against the wetness of her pussy lips. The contact was sweet enough to push her close to orgasm. But she deliberately curtailed that response.

With the final button fastened, the tailor drew a heavy breath and stepped back to admire her. There was no trace of lechery in his expression. His gaze was the critical examination she expected from a professional admiring his work and checking for imperfections or errors. She stood rigid beneath his gaze, holding her breath, not daring to move, and basking in the glory of her new coat and all the sensations it evoked.

"Take a look in the mirror," the tailor suggested.

His avuncular hand again fell to her arm and he guided her to the corner of the shop where he kept a cheval mirror.

With the flick of a switch she was bathed in the beams of brilliant fluorescence. The light was so intense it stung her retinas.

Linda blinked her vision clear and studied the reflection. Her delight was so strong it brought her close to the point of orgasm. The leather made her body look like perfection personified. It smoothed over her hips and breasts. Flowing down to the floor it combined elegance and sophistication with something far more sultry and derivative. It was the perfect look she had wanted to achieve and her chest swelled with pride and satisfaction.

The pressure against her breasts tightened.

Her nipples were crushed beneath the constraints of the coat.

She released a sigh, wary that breathing too heavily would push her beyond the brink of climax. Stealing a hand over her chest she shivered as the sensitive flesh beneath the leather responded to her touch. The inner muscles of her sex clenched and convulsed with their own thrill of mounting euphoria.

"I can't see the need for any immediate adjustments," the tailor murmured.

She had forgotten he was in the room. Glancing at him, watching him adjust his spectacles and study her myopically, she said, "It's perfect."

He grinned and raised a questioning eyebrow. "You're satisfied?"

She shook her head and reached for the button at her throat. "Not yet," she admitted. "But I don't think that will be a problem with this coat." She left the statement hanging between them as she opened the button at her throat and peeled it from her neck.

The collar had pressed against her windpipe. Once it was unfastened she was able to draw a long breath. Her chest rose. The sensation of the silk lining caressing her nipples became unbearable. Her fingers trembled as she reached for the second and third buttons. The pressure was removed from her breasts but, each time her chest rose or fell, the coat diligently stroked her breasts. She could feel herself growing weak with the need to climax and knew, regardless of whether or not the tailor was watching, she had to allow herself the indulgence.

The fourth and fifth buttons allowed a wave of cool air to slide between her flesh and the lining of the coat. Linda hadn't realized a film of perspiration coated her body. It was only when the mellow chill touched her skin that she understood the intensity of her arousal.

Hurriedly she unfastened the final two buttons.

The lapels of the coat peeled apart to reveal her pale flesh cloaked in glorious black leather. Her fingers lingered near the crease of her sex. She could detect the heat radiating from her pussy and knew it would only take a careful caress and ecstasy would be hers. She fixed her gaze on the woman in the mirror, admiring her boldness, her exhibitionism and her coat.

From the corner of her eye she saw the tailor grin with approval.

And then she was touching herself.

Her fingers went to the smooth, shaved split of her sex and she clutched herself tightly. One finger slid between the lips of her sex. The others did nothing more than press against her outer labia. But the sensation of flesh on flesh—the same sensation that came from touching and wearing the new coat—was enough to release her climax.

Linda threw her head back and roared.

Pounding waves of satisfaction thundered through her body. The orgasm was a cataclysmic release of every contained impulse she had ever suppressed. Her muscles turned limp as the shock of pure joy breached her senses. The brilliant lights above the cheval mirror grew brighter before they started to fade with her consciousness.

The tailor appeared by her side and held her arm. His presence was enough to steady her as the final thrill of the orgasm wracked her body. Without him she knew she would have collapsed and fallen to the floor. Glancing at the front of his pants, expecting to see he was still aroused and sporting an unsightly bulge, she smiled when she noticed the damp stain of his ejaculation.

He asked, "You're happy with the coat?"

"I think that's an understatement," she grinned.

He nodded. His demeanor was, as always, acutely professional. "Then, if we can sort out the remainder of the balance owed, I shall wrap the coat for you."

Linda shook her head and clutched defensively at the lapels. "If you could wrap the clothes I was wearing when I arrived, I'll wear this now."

He handed her a bag and she saw it already contained her possessions. "I thought you might say that," he grinned.

And, in that moment, she realized that one day soon, regardless of how well the new coat served her, she would return to the tailor's shop. The thought was almost as warming as the leather that clung to her bare flesh.

As she settled her account, Linda thought that if she encountered any arrogant university students on the return journey, she would tell them that Truman Capote had been wrong: dressing up for masturbation made the experience far more satisfying.

JUDE MASON

THOSE BOOTS

LIGHT-HEADED, MESMERIZED, Max couldn't take his eyes off them. The white leather stiletto boots with their five-inch heels and the toe that would de-nut a bull if he were kicked in just the right way. Gawd, they were amazing.

He took a step closer to the red-brick storefront, suddenly aware of the traffic noises behind him. It was rush hour and somehow he'd lost the deafening sound of it. Glancing around, sure everyone would be staring at him, he was pleasantly surprised to see crowds blissfully ignoring him, and each other, in their scramble to get home.

He must be insane. But he couldn't help himself. He didn't have a choice; he had to.

They'd go over his knees. He imagined how they'd feel, crushing his toes together. Walking would be next to impossible, but that just added to his excitement. The leather would fit snuggly around his calves, loose at the ankles. The tops would sag down and bulge around his thighs, where they'd rub the more sensitive flesh, maybe even pull a little, or slap when he walked. He loved that. The pristine white of the boots: he'd never seen anything so sexy, so in-your-face sexy.

His upper lip felt moist. He was sweating. Suddenly, his suit jacket was stifling. Sweat trickled down his sides, itched. His cock pressed hard against his slacks.

He slid his right hand into his pocket and readjusted himself. He looked around again, checking, hoping no one was watching. His face grew hot. What if someone saw him? Would it make a difference?

Sheepishly, he looked into the shopwindow again, eyes immediately going to the boots. One standing tall, obviously something had been shoved down inside to hold it straight. The other stood beside it, toe turned out, showing that amazing heel and the curve of the instep. At the knee, it flopped over the other; the long tube of leather collapsed together, waiting for a toe to slip inside, separate it, and fill it out.

"Fuck!" he breathed, feeling his shaft swell, his balls churn. His hand, still in his pocket, still gripping his cock, tightened. He closed his eyes, trying to block out the vision of those sensuous, beautiful boots. At first, the pleasure was almost too much and he had to hold his breath or explode, but when he tightened his grip even more, the pleasure vanished and an ache took over. Ache turned to pain. His erection faded, and he exhaled slowly.

The urge was still there, just under the surface. When he opened his eyes, he was at the door, his free hand on the brass knob. He stopped.

The knob was cold, his fingers tightened around it. A deep breath cleared his head, but not much. He turned the knob. It stuck; he cranked a little harder, suddenly desperate to get inside.

The hinge squealed. A bell rang. The smell of leather was like a warm blanket, wrapping him in a fantasy. Sweet, earthy, musky, animal, the odor tickled his nose and slid over his tongue.

Once he'd taken a step inside and let the door go, it slammed shut with a finality that jarred him out of his silent enthrallment. He blinked, and gazed around the small shop. To his left, rows of bags lined the wall: purses, satchels, and various carryalls. Everything was leather, and each carried that luscious smell he so adored.

To his right, almost within reach, were the women's shoes. Boxes, all colors and sizes, stacked against the wall from the floor to nearly waist height. Above them were the displays—heels, sandals, boots, runners, every kind of shoe a woman could possibly desire—each shown to its best advantage on tiny glass shelves running from the top of the boxes to the ceiling.

He felt as if the air was alive. The scent intoxicated him. His clothes smothered him. It was then he realized his hand was still thrust deeply into his pocket and his fingers were lightly running up and down the throbbing shaft of his cock. The squeeze to slow his lust hadn't lasted long, not nearly as long as he'd hoped it would. A last caress and he pulled his hand out.

The room was suddenly sweltering. Sliding his jacket off, he tossed it over the nearest chair. A long line of chairs covered with red leather upholstery ran down the center of the shop. Footrests sat perched in front of each chair, just waiting for customers.

His heart thundered in his chest. He scanned the store and there was no one around. Dare he? Could he brave his way through it? His prick throbbed lustily against his slacks.

He took a few tentative steps toward the boots, those boots. His senses reeled. The scent of leather grew stronger, his erection more urgent with each step he took. He had to stop. His vision blurred, his hand returned to his cock, but this time over his slacks. As soon as he palmed the swollen, aching shaft, it pulsed. The inside of his shorts was sticky with precome and felt wonderful sliding across the glans.

He took a deep, shuddering breath, and nearly swooned at the heady scent. It gave him the strength to take another few steps forward though, and that landed him in front of the window, in front of his boots.

His. He'd begun to think of them as his.

"May I help you?"

Max spun, caught. Heart pounding, hand forgotten, he stood gaping.

She was gorgeous. Short, couldn't be more than five-two, curves where it counted and more; luscious, dark blonde hair framed a face that made him think *elfin*. Best of all, she was clad in leather from chin to toe. Pale tan, soft, exquisitely tailored to hug her curves; the dress had obviously been made for her. It clung to her, as if it was her skin, her flesh from the neck down to her hips. Then, it flared gracefully to the floor where impossibly pointed brown leather toes peeked out from beneath the hem.

Her voice had been deep, sultry, sensual. God, he loved voices like that.

He opened his mouth. Nothing came out but air.

She stood there smiling, as if waiting for him to compose himself, or leave, or fade into the ether. Putting one hand on a hip, she cocked her head and made no effort to rescue him.

Max swallowed, and tried again. This time, he managed a croak. "Boots. White leather ones."

"Ah, yes, the stilettos." She approached him. How simple that sounded, but how much more difficult it seemed as he watched her. She undulated beneath her skirt. He'd never seen someone undulate before, but he could think of no other way to describe her movement. And it was amazing to watch. Her tits went one way; the leather almost went with them, but not quite. Her hips swayed, wide handfuls of hips. The skirt hugged them, but couldn't quite sway as much and slid across her flesh.

Eyes glued to her hips, then her tits, he croaked, "Yes." He tightened his grip. Realized with sudden shock he'd just squeezed his cock in front of her and pulled his hand away. His face burned with embarrassment. Escape crossed his mind, but she was between him and the door.

"You want to see the boots?"

He knew she was struggling not to laugh. He saw it in her face, when he dared raise his eyes. Saw it when she took a deep breath, and then exhaled. Her chest, her tits, jiggled with a stifled chuckle.

He inhaled. Leather, musk, delicious scent transported the shame. "Yes, I want to see them."

"Let me lock the door."

Confused, he watched her turn and go toward the door. Her ass, firm, round, was like two puppies snuggling against each other as she walked away from him. She turned the deadbolt. He was trapped. He could scarcely get a breath.

She turned and looked at him calmly. "You'll have trouble trying these on with those slacks."

"Huh?" His brain was so befuddled, he couldn't think of anything but her and the boots.

"Take off your slacks." She walked past him, hooking the white leather boots out of the window when she passed them. His nose followed her, inhaling, tracking, wanting to touch and taste, to rub himself against her soft curves.

So casual, so nonthreatening. So outrageous. But his hand crept out from behind him and went to his belt buckle. Pulled, opened; next was the button holding them closed, and then the zipper. A whir and it was down. His cock bulged through the opening.

"Come." She patted the chair nearest the back of the shop. "Sit here, you'll be more comfortable."

In a trance, drunk with lust and need, he shuffled forward. His slacks eased down over his hips, past his thighs. He grabbed hold, but knew he must look ridiculous shambling across the empty expanse toward her. He didn't care—couldn't have stopped if he had. Reaching her, he stopped. His eyes roamed the leather-clad curves only inches away. He smelled her sweat mixed with the cowhide's aroma.

"Good boy. Now drop them and sit here." Her voice had taken on a much sterner tone. But even that didn't matter. Her instructions were exactly what he needed. His fingers opened, and his slacks slid down his legs and pooled around his ankles.

He sat in the chair she'd indicated, and leaned down to slip out of his shoes. Leather, brown oxfords, the smell, the feel—his cock pulsed against his belly. He pushed his pants off, and put them on the chair beside him, crumpled, unnecessary.

When he sat up straight, she was there, inches from him, her hip level with his face. His breath came in ragged gasps. Could he touch her, the dress, feel its leather softness? His hand rose, reached, but was slapped away. "Naughty. Take off your socks."

He sucked in a breath. She knew. She knew it all.

The socks joined his slacks. Unnecessary, scrunched up, turned inside out, and ignored. He wriggled his toes. Stretched his legs out and sighed as the cool air caressed his feet.

"Remove your shirt and underpants." Her voice had grown harsher, more demanding. He loved it.

He rose and worked the buttons loose on his shirt, fighting them, nearly tearing the soft cotton before he shed the offending garment onto the growing pile of clothing. He stopped then, for a moment. His erection ached, throbbed dully. Looking down, he saw a wet circle of darker material where precome had soaked into the brushed cotton.

"Do it, now!"

He glanced at her face; saw the determination there, the lust. Slipping his fingers into the waistband—his trembling, sweat-covered fingers—he pushed them down. As he bent, his body covered his crotch, hid his embarrassingly erect prick from her view. But when he'd tossed his shorts onto the pile, he had to stand, to show himself, and expose his lust.

He leaned forward. His nose brushed her thigh. Soft, sensual, animal hide took his breath. Max stood up straight, fists clenched at his sides to keep from covering his erection, and faced her.

"I know what you're thinking, little man. I know who sent you. I know what you want," she sneered at him, then scanned down his body. With one long blood-red nail, she tapped the head of his cock, making it bounce. "This wants to play." She tapped it again, and he groaned. "This needs leather to play with." Taking firm hold of his shaft, she looked into his eyes and asked, "Am I right?"

"Yes, Ma'am." He couldn't keep eye contact. Ashamed, he lowered his head.

"Good boy." She gave his cock a gentle squeeze and then released it. "Your wife must love you a lot to send you here."

Shocked, he dared to look at her again, but instantly regretted it. Her snarling, "Don't you dare look into my eyes again without me telling you to," caught him completely off guard.

He gasped, and dropped his gaze. With his pulse pounding in his ears, excited beyond anything he'd felt before, he stood waiting for her to command him. "I'm sorry, Ma'am. It won't happen again."

"Now then, sit down and put on the boots."

Just the words were almost enough to send him skyrocketing to orgasm. If she touched him again, he'd shoot. Neither of those things happened, but when she uttered her next words, it almost didn't matter. "And don't you dare come without my permission."

"Oh, God," he moaned before he could stop. The head of his cock was purple, the eye oozing clear nectar, which hung like a strand of diamonds from the tip. The veins pulsed along the shaft, blood racing, urging him to explode. Balls, taut and ready, climbed even higher, nearly disappearing under the shaft. A touch, a breath would have been too much. Somehow, he managed to control himself, to stave off that ultimate release of pleasure.

"Boots. Put them on." She raised her hand, poised a finger above his cockhead, but didn't strike, no matter how much he wanted her to. "I won't repeat myself again."

He dropped into the seat, reveling in the slick chill of the leather, and reached for the boots she'd set on the floor at her side. The leather creaked under him, his legs spread and his sack touching the chair. Breathless with excitement, he continued. The moment his fingers connected with the soft cuff of the boot, felt the soft warmth of the hide against his fingertips, he thought he might faint. Light-headed, his skin tingling, he brought the boot closer. He wrapped his hand more firmly around the tall leg, unwilling to take the chance of dropping his prize.

He leaned back in the chair. Cold leather pressed against his back. He inhaled. Raising his foot, opening the gaping maw that was his entrance into the footwear, he poised—posed—breathed the beauty of the experience, before allowing his toe to connect.

Toe slid in, his instep rubbed against the soft hide, the upper plane of his foot brushed, then slid down into the tube of leather. Leather smell encircled his face. Soft hide bent and caressed his skin, both hand and foot, as he eased his toe deeper. Encountering the heel of the boot, he smiled and bent his foot, pushing more firmly, pulling with his hands. Ankle held snug, calf surrounded by the sweet softness; he groaned and strained for control. Knee and inner thigh held, firmly teased and caressed, by the hide.

Not yet, he prayed to his silent goddess of tanned hide. Too soon, he wasn't ready. One more to go. He took a moment to compose himself. He sat back, extended his leg, and raised his foot, its booted sheath covering a delight to his senses.

"Nice," the woman, his tormentress, expounded. "The other now."

Although he was unsure of his ability to complete the task without climaxing, Max nonetheless moved to comply. Boot in hand, the shaft of his cock squeezed tight between thigh and belly, he eased his toe in. The nail of his big toe scraped along the leather interior. He readjusted his grip, and shook out the long tube of hide, then pushed his foot deep.

"Ah," he sighed, when his inner calf rubbed the skin; goose bumps raced up his leg, more rose on his chest and crept up his neck. He shuddered. He clenched his ass. His balls churned and shifted.

Heel touched, toe lifted and foot pushed deep into the white stiletto. The arch of his foot ached, matching its twin on the other side. A final push, and then he smoothed the leg. From ankle to shin, to knee then thigh, one then the other, caressed and cajoled, until he was beside himself with the need to stroke his cock.

Done, and beyond ecstatic, he placed his feet on the floor, one beside the other, ankles touching; he admired the way they looked. Leather scent wafted around him, rich, sultry, perfection. He placed each hand on a knee. Leather clad, sleek, soft; take a breath and feel the hide.

"Good boy." Her voice interrupted his pleasure. "Sit up straight and spread your knees."

By then, he was trembling. He eased his knees apart and straightened his back, but couldn't keep still. His inner thighs quivered and sent his cock swaying back and forth. His calves felt stretched tight from the posture forced by the heels. His toes were crushed together.

The smell of his own lust mixed with the leather was more than he'd expected, almost more than he could bear. He clenched his hands on his thighs to keep from stroking his cock.

When she moved forward, he knew she had other plans and he couldn't stop the whimper that escaped. Stepping between his thighs, her leather-clad leg brushed against his cock. His body jerked.

"Kiss my belly," she whispered in a voice that dripped dominance. But when he leaned forward, to his amazement and excitement, his cock rubbed against the top of the boots he wore. His shuddering escalated with each heartbeat. His lips pressed to her leather-encased belly. He inhaled. Slick and warm from both her body and his breath, the leather scent was like a cocoon.

"And here," she whispered, touching a spot next to where he'd just kissed.

Max shifted slightly, and gasped. Excitement soared as his cockhead dragged across the leather and his face pressed against her belly. He'd never been so close to coming, yet managed to hold off. He pinched his thigh, the pain helping him focus on anything but the leather and his relentless surging pleasure.

"And here," she cooed, placing her finger a hairbreadth from the last spot.

"Please..." The word, the beginnings of a plea for mercy came before he was aware of its presence.

"Here"—more firmly, more insistent came her demand.

Sobbing, he eased himself to the side. Cock pulsed, balls churned—a droplet of precome oozed and tickled and tormented him as it slid across the supersensitive glans. He pressed his lips to the leather.

Luscious, delicious, smooth-to-the-touch, heavenly scented animal hide slick with his sweat slid against his lips.

He flicked his tongue across her belly, tasting his sweat and the tang of leather. His cock lurched. He moaned, terrified he'd come without permission. Her fingers slid through his hair, gripped, and then pulled his face away from the wonderful, evil hide he so lusted after.

He squirmed, but she pulled harder and he immediately stopped when his cock pulsed and pulsed again. Too close, too fucking close.

"Leather freak." Her voice was like warm honey, smooth and soft, the words like a badge he must wear. "Come for me. Rub your cock against me. Wrap your arms around me and come."

Words he'd longed to hear. It took but a second to slide forward, perching his ass closer to the front of the slick red chair, his cock more firmly against her—her and the luscious leather skin covering flesh. The underside of his cockhead slid up her leg and he sucked air in through clenched teeth. His hips jerked, needing to fuck. He wrapped his arms around her waist—buried his face against the soft slickness between her breasts. As he was inhaling, swooning with pleasure, his hips jerked again. His cock pulsed, throbbed, and swelled. Precome oiled the route his cock found and he thrust against her firmness. Lust fired him. The scent of her body mixed with the leather stretched taut across her breasts nudged him a step closer to orgasm.

Balls churned, his cock pulsed wildly. Blind with passion, he focused on the rhythmic pulsing in his cock and the come rising along its shaft, his climax teased closer. He gulped, then held his breath, body straining against itself, the leather pressing against him. An exploding, gut-wrenching release gripped and held him. His heartbeat drummed in his ears. A pulse, and a stream of hot come spewed between them. Leather slicked with it, belly anointed with his spunk. A ragged breath, an inhaled tang of leather, then he shot again, groaning at the painful, wonderful pleasure tearing into him.

He gasped, and rubbed his face against her breasts, soft breasts, leather covered and luscious. A final shudder, a final pulse, and he sighed.

Her hand was on the back of his neck, stroking him easily. "Beautiful," she murmured and moved her hips side to side, spreading his come and sweat. "Shower?"

Max looked up at her, grateful, exhausted. "Please." He sagged back in the chair and realized that his feet were killing him. His toes and arches weren't used to being so mistreated. He loved it.

"In the back room, you know where."

"Thank you." He reached out, grabbed her hand and brought it to his lips. Kissing her fingertips, he looked up and felt a blush heat his face. "You always know how to make me mad for you."

His wife of thirteen years looked down at him and replied, "And you know how to turn me on like no one else." She stroked his cheek and smiled. "Come shower with me."

The door remained locked while she helped him pull off the boots they both loved.

TSAURAH LITZKY

LOVE IS LONG

LOVE IS LONG, I thought as he walked toward me down the bar to get my drink order.

Love must be ten inches, eight inches, at the very least, I estimated as I looked at the cylindrical bulge down his thigh beneath his tight jeans. I raised my eyes to his face. He had large glittering eyes, so dark they looked black, a fierce hawk nose, big lush pink lips. His black hair was drawn back to the nape of his neck and tied with a leather cord that looped down on either side of his shoulders. He was wearing striking leather accessories: a thick mahogany leather belt with a fine silver buckle and on his wrists, brown leather cuffs embossed with an intricate black pattern.

I was on a hunt, and he would do very well indeed. I wanted some skin, some hot man skin to soothe my aching heart, to blanket my dejected body, to penetrate deep within me and thrill me where I begin.

My lover, Lucian, had just left the country, his student visa expired. He had asked me if I would marry him so he could stay. "We can divorce later," he said. "It would just be doing a little favor for a friend." I knew then, contrary to all my hopes, that he would never love me. I told him no. He thanked me for the few laughs we'd shared and told me I made the best pasta primavera he had ever tasted. Now he is in Germany visiting an old girlfriend and I am in the Buccaneer Bar hoping for a score good enough to reassure me that I am still beautiful.

"What can I get you?" the sexy bartender asks, standing in front of me. Before I answer, I lean forward to give him a good view of the ample cleavage exposed by the deep V-neck of my favorite red dress. I smile up at him in what I hope is a fetching manner. "Belvedere and tonic, easy on the ice," I tell him. "And make it a double."

"You like the best," he says and smiles at me approvingly. While he is fixing my drink I put a twenty on the bar to pay but when he brings the drink, he won't take any money. "The first one is on the house," he says.

I watch him as he works. His movements are fluid and quick as a dancer's. His shirtsleeves are rolled up to his elbows and the thick leather cuffs he is wearing show off the powerful sinews of his arms. He chats with two women wearing black dresses and lots of makeup. He makes them laugh.

Three big guys, loud and boisterous in rugby uniforms, come in. While he is getting their beers, the tallest one looks down the bar and waves at me, gestures to me to come over. If he's not man enough to come over, he's not man enough for me, but I don't care. I have a crush on Mr. Leather Cuffs. The drink he made me is so delicious. I try to visualize Lucian's face but find I cannot. So what if he is in a Munich beer hall canoodling with some Valkyrie. I am floating in a vodka cloud in the best bar in South Brooklyn with my red dress on and…

"Enjoying your drink?" he asks. I was so engrossed in my own happy thoughts, I didn't realize Mr. Leather Cuffs was approaching.

I struggle to come back to planet Earth. "It's great," I tell him, "just what the doctor ordered."

"You don't look sick in that beautiful red dress," he says, "you look gorgeous, like you're celebrating. So, what is it you're celebrating?"

I summon what courage I can and go for it. "Freedom, it's freedom I'm celebrating," I say. He licks his lips and I see his tongue for the first time, fleshy and thick like a little cock. I think of that cock inside me and suddenly I'm nervous so I start to prattle.

"I can't help but notice those striking leather cuffs you're wearing. What is that writing on them? Are those symbols or letters?"

He tells me the symbols are Sanskrit letters. "*All or nothing* is what they say." Then he asks me if I like leather.

I tell him, "I love leather," although really I don't have any experience with leather at all.

He licks his lips again. "Oh, yeah," he says. "Well then, I get off at ten and it's nine thirty now. Want to come home with me and see my leather collection?" I want to be sassy and ask him how he came up with such an original line but even more I want that big tongue locked with mine so I just say, "Yes."

In the taxi from the bar to his loft in Greenpoint I find out his name is Roger and I tell him my name is Roberta. I don't like the name Roger so I tell him I'd rather call him Mr. Leather Cuffs. He says all right then, he'll call me Miss Red Dress. He is wearing some kind of leathery cologne that is so pungent it makes my head spin. The taxi is going very fast, speeding through the night, careening around the corners at breakneck speed.

Suddenly, I feel dizzy like I'm on the roller coaster in Coney Island. What have I let myself in for? I barely know this mysterious Mr. Leather Cuffs. What if his collection is a collection of leather whips? What if he wants to use every one of them on me? I want to run away as we exit the taxi, yet I do not. It is as if he exerts a magnetic pull on me. Still my qualms keep me silent as we ride up in the elevator to his place on the top floor.

"Don't worry, Miss Red Dress, I would never hurt you," he says as if reading my mind. He unlocks the door, ushers me in, closes the door behind us and turns on the light. We are in a large white room furnished with a black leather couch and a couple of yellow leather armchairs. A beat-up old trunk in front of the couch serves as a coffee table. Large windows run along one wall. He gestures to the wall next to it.

"My collection," he says. I am looking at a stunning array of leather masks and hoods in varying sizes and colors, black, white, red, purple, shocking pink. Some are studded or decorated with paint or feathers.

"Do you like my collection?" he asks.

"Very much," I tell him. I have never seen anything like it. "Did you ever make love wearing a leather hood or mask?" he asks.

"No," I answer. I did once do it with Cliff Gerstenhaber when I was wearing my black movie star sunglasses and Cliff was wearing his Yankees cap but I don't tell Mr. Leather Cuffs that.

"Now you're going to have your chance," he says, "but let's have a drink first."

I study the hoods and masks while he mixes the drinks in a small alcove fixed up as a kitchen. We down our drinks quickly, and then he puts the Rolling Stones on the stereo.

He tells me to choose something. I select a black harlequin mask with exaggerated cat's eyes, which just covers my nose but leaves my mouth exposed and ready for anything.

"I approve your choice," he says. "Now I'm going to take you into my bedroom. Take off all your clothes, your shoes, everything, then lie down on the bed and wait for me." He leads me through a high door into a windowless room that contains a big bed covered with a deer-skin, a dresser and a full-length mirror that runs the length of one wall.

I strip as he told me, put my things on top of the dresser, then tie on the mask. Once again, I am immersed in the aroma of leather, leather so soft it seems to blend with my skin. The mask was designed in such a way that it fits perfectly over my almond eyes.

I go look at myself in the mirror. I am transformed. I am an exotic wood nymph, my long blonde hair streaming out from beneath the mask. My lips are thicker and my eyes sparkle with a new green light. My pendulous breasts sway slightly as if beckoning, calling out *touch me, suck me*. I lie down on the bed and try to assume what I hope is a seductive pose. The mask already seems melded into me, part of my head.

He steps into the room, his head half-covered by a simple black hood that conceals his hair and the top of his face. The hood has large pointy ears. He is nude except for that mahogany belt around his waist. He has taken off the leather cuffs and donned a pair of rough brown leather gloves that look like buckskin. His hair is still gathered up by that same black leather cord knotted at the back of his neck. The purple tube of flesh between his legs is semierect and even longer than I expected, supernaturally long, making him look like some kind of primitive satyr out of a mythology book.

I stutter out the first thing that comes into my head. "You're not wearing your cuffs, I can't call you Mr. Leather Cuffs anymore."

"You can call me Leather Man," he says. "You're a gift for my eyes. Now, I want to caress you, I want to caress you in a very special leather man way, but first you must let me tie your arms behind you with my belt."

Once again I am apprehensive, but I nod yes. He opens the belt, takes it off and asks me to turn over on my belly and cross my wrists behind me. He loops the belt around my wrists and fastens it. The leather is surprisingly soft and smooth and feels like satin against my skin.

He turns me over and starts to slowly rub his gloved hands, his leather hands, all over my body. The feeling of the rough leather at my waist, on my rib cage, inside my thighs is intensely pleasurable. He reaches down and grabs my nipples with his leather fingers, pulling at them at first gently but then more roughly, rolling them between his fingers in a way that sends ripples of desire out into every corner of my body.

My nipples rest between his wedding ring fingers and his fuck-you fingers. He squeezes these fingers together, then he lifts his hands. The nipples follow pulling the rest of the tit up, up, up. My body turns inside out and I became a total pulsing vacuum wanting him. I wanted his leather inside me more then anything.

"Please, please, Leather Man, fuck me, fuck me," I beg.

"Not yet," he answers. He unties the leather cord that is holding his hair back. His glossy mane falls like a curtain on either side of his head. He moves, positioning himself between my legs. He holds the leather cord straight between his fingers, threading it back and forth inside my sex, stitching me, sewing me, stirring me into a frenzy. My body rocks from side to side as he works me with the leather thread. Just as I am about to come, he stops. He holds the cord up to my nostrils.

"Do you like the smell of leather love?" he asks.

"I want more," I gasp.

He puts the cord between my lips. "Suck on the cord while Leather Man fucks you," he says. He makes me come so many times I lose count.

We lie side by side sated. He has taken off his hood and my mask and unbelted my wrists. My arm rests across his chest. His hand strokes the pelt between my legs. The leather cord is jumbled up beside me on the bed. I pick it up.

"What are you going to do with this?" I ask, grinning. "I don't think you can use it again."

"No," he agrees. "You keep it to remember the first night you met Leather Man."

I smile as I wrap the cord around my wrist, a leather convert after all.

ALISON TYLER

HIDE

LEATHER. I have always loved the smell of leather, the feel of it on my skin. There is something insanely sexual about the texture; the way, after years of wear, it molds to the owner's body. Perhaps it's the Neanderthal left in me, the cave girl clad in a mountain lion's hide, but wearing skins makes me feel more alive.

For myself, I choose sleek leather pants and riding boots, a leather vest worn open over a white T-shirt. On a lover, I like to see a black leather jacket cut close to the body, thigh-high leather boots pulled over opaque black stockings, and nothing, or very little, in between. I like to stroke a woman's skin through the skin, her hide through the hide; testing the dangerous give in the texture, the supple caress; breathing in the sinful scent, the medley of near-intoxicating odors.

My love for leather has lasted close to twenty years, since I bought my first motorcycle and its accompanying biker jacket. And despite a

Harvard education and an inclination toward writing poetry, my fixation has become my means of employment: I own a leather goods store in the hip part of L.A., on Melrose Avenue.

At thirty-seven, I'm older than the kids who walk down the strip in racer-back tank tops and baggy jeans, younger than the matrons who glare as they drive by in their Jaguars and Saabs. About the same age as the woman who walked into my place in the middle of a slow day, a Wednesday afternoon.

She was stunning, just my type: long legs, red hair falling in loose curls past her shoulders, golden-green eyes that flashed at me in the late afternoon light. She strode into my store like a lioness on the prowl, the smell of her prey teasing her, making her fine nostrils flare as she moved up and down the aisles. I watched her from my perch behind the counter; watched as she touched the skimpy, pounded-leather dresses, ran her fingers along the smooth jackets, the shiny slacks.

I watched her, but I didn't say anything.

There are some customers who come in looking to buy clothes that will make them look cool. I recognize the posers, the Hollywood Rocker set, who belong to the young L.A. crowd. They're happening only because they're young and in L.A. These jokers snag the vinyl jeans, the butt-hugging suede, the thigh-high microminis. Others, my raunchy sex-fiends, buy shiny black chaps, cutaway dresses, unbelievably short shorts, bras and bikinis studded with silver. They spare no expense to buy what it takes to make them come, and I cull most of my money from them.

But I wait for, and wish for, and fantasize about the she-tigers, the lady lions, the ones, like this redhead, who need the feel of the hide on their naked skin. Need the scent of it caressing their lovely bodies.

These customers are the ones I opened my shop, Hide, for in the first place, and they are the beauties I wait for.

And watch.

She had on a mint green halter top that made her eyes glow the same color, and cutoff jeans that showed me a bit of her panties when she bent to look at the boots lined on the wall. Her ass made me dizzy, the way it filled out those shorts, the way the faded denim hugged her sweet tail. She was a beauty, a thoroughbred. A prize.

"Do you have this in a sex?" she asked softly, startling me from my daydreams of what she'd look like in a black leather jacket, fishnets, and black motorcycle boots. Startling me from a picture of her tied down to my bed with all my leather gear in place and a pair of stiff scissors in my hand.

"A *six*?" she repeated, moving closer to the counter. I saw that look in her eyes, the look of the huntress, the look of the goddess, and I nodded, quickly, and motioned for her to follow me to the back.

She did, high-heeled sandals clicking on the wood floor, and I opened the door and ushered her in, spreading my arms to show her my private collection.

"Ohhh." A sigh. She had found Nirvana.

"Your size," I said huskily. "Everything. All of it. Try on any piece you want." She went quickly to the first rack, her long red nails stroking the sides of the lace-up pants, her palms caressing the velvety soft insides of the jackets, the butter-soft leather, black as midnight, some pieces shiny, others worn with age and love.

"Where?" she asked, looking around the room. There are mirrors on the walls, but no private dressing room in the back.

"You can use the rooms out front," I told her. "Or change right here."

She shot me a look, one that made me melt. "Here's fine."

In a second, her green top was on the floor, her shorts next, and panties last—no bra, she didn't need one—and she was into the first outfit before I could fully register the concept of her body. The skin, the hide, sliding against her pale, naked body, turned me on more than anything I could possibly imagine, more than simply staring at her nude form could have done. She'd chosen one of my favorites, right from the beginning, a pair of tight black riding pants and a matching vest, worn over nothing but her pale, creamy skin. She slid into her sandals then swung her hair out of the way to catch her reflection in the mirror.

"That was made for you," I mumbled.

She nodded, more to her mirror image than to my statement, and stared at herself in the critical way that I've noticed even very pretty women do. That look never appears on my own face. I'm secure in my body, in the strength of it, the lines of it, but that may be because of my years or because my father treated both his daughters and sons alike. We were given no special treatment, no coddling. When I look in the mirror I don't see a painted picture, a gilded reflection. I see straight to my soul.

She wasn't sure, wasn't totally satisfied, and she kicked off the shoes, peeled down the slacks and went rifling through the racks, clad only in the leather top, showing me all of her charms, her golden-furred pussy when she turned my way, her pink pussy lips when she bent over.

"Do you like that?" I asked as she reached for a dress, one with laces at the sides and back. It was a dress made for a motorcycle-lady, made as specifically for this woman as if she had been the designer's muse.

She slipped off the vest for an answer, sliding the dress over her head and then stalking toward me and turning, wanting me to fasten the laces in back. I did it with shaking hands, moving her long hair out of the way so that I could do it right. She was tall, at least five-ten in bare feet, and the dress fit her like a leather glove. She moved away as soon as I was done with the laces, sidling up to the mirror and then pirouetting in front of it.

She liked this one better. I could tell. The way she pursed her lips at her image, the way she moved a few feet back and looked down, her chin tilted at an angle, taking in her entire reflected twin.

"You could try it with fringe boots," I suggested, unsure of how much input she wanted. She seemed to be on a mission, and if she were buying to please a lover, I'd have to watch my step.

"Yeah," she looked at me expectantly. "What do you have?"

I rushed to get the highest pair from the rack out front and grabbed my favorite motorcycle boots, as well. While I was nearby, I shut and locked the front door, turning the OUT TO LUNCH sign face forward.

When I returned, she was still standing in front of the mirror, but now she had on a pair of fishnet hose, snagged from one of the inventory boxes. "Hope it's okay," she said, giving me a different kind of look with those lake green eyes.

"Sure." *Anything you want,* unsaid, but implied. I handed over the boots and she slid them on. Again, a perfect fit. She walked a few steps forward and a few steps back, almost doing a dance. Then she turned to face me.

"What do you think?"

Did she want a salesperson's opinion, or one of a lust-filled admirer?

"You're stunning," I said, my husky baritone going down another octave. But I was quick to correct myself, my mind working instantly. "I mean, it looks stunning on you." I've never been one to stutter. As I said, I have always felt confident with my dark looks, confident in the lean, sturdy weight of my body, but this woman made me shake.

"Yes," she turned to regard the mirror again. "I like this one best."

I pulled together my nerve. "Is it for a special occasion?"

"No. Just for myself. I needed a lift. And leather always makes me feel…sexy. Something about the scent, the smell of it."

I nodded.

"You understand," she asked, "don't you?"

"It's why I have the store," I told her, wanting to touch her, restraining myself from taking her in my arms and stroking her through the soft leather, feeling the place, the wondrous place where her skin ended and the hide began. The leather and the skin, the hide on the hide. Circling it, sniffing it, getting down on the floor and pressing my face to her body, wrapping my arms around her waist and smelling *her* animal scent through the musky odor of the hide.

"What's your name?" she asked then, breaking me from my day-dreams.

"Patrice." My voice sounded so deep to my own ears. Deep and filled with longing. I wanted to own her.

"I'm Diana."

Of course she was. Diana, goddess of the moon. The queen and the huntress.

She walked a step closer, clicking in those fringed boots. "Why do you keep all of the best back here?"

The honest reason is that I don't want it to appear on just anyone. You need to love leather to wear it right. I've only found a few people I considered worthy of owning the best. This lady was definitely one of them.

"I don't like to waste it."

Now she was the one to nod. Another step closer. "Patrice?"

"Yeah."

"Do you want to feel?"

Another step.

I bowed my head. *Was she teasing me?* "Yeah."

She moved quickly then, into my arms, and I rested my head on her shoulder and breathed in the smell of her body, right at the underside of her neck, that secret, haunting she-woman smell. Then, with her scent still tickling my nose, I went down to my knees and pressed my lips to her sex, kissing her here, smelling her here, getting wave upon wave of the mingling perfumes, the leather and the lady, the sweet smell of the old leather, the fresh scent of the woman.

I stroked her body through the skin, dragging my palms firmly along the sleek lines of her hips, over her thighs. She moved away from me, dancing away, sliding free from the dress and returning to the rack, completely nude, choosing another pair of pants and a tight jacket with zippered sleeves. She never took her eyes off me as she pulled on the pants, wriggled into the jacket. She zipped into the second pair of boots, the cycle ones. Then she came back, wanting me to feel her again.

I grabbed her lower this time, moving my hands down her calves to her ankles. Holding her tightly here, through two layers of leather, the slacks and the boots. Gripping into her body firmly enough so that she could feel my strength. My desire. In my mind, I could hear a poem (hundreds of years old), that could have been written for her specifically. A poem for a huntress:

Lay thy bow of pearl apart.
And thy crystal-shining quiver;
Give unto the flying heart
Space to breathe, how short soever
Thou that mak'st a day of night,
Goddess excellently bright.

I suddenly knew what it would be like to have her riding behind me on my Harley, her arms tight around my own waist. Knew what it would be like to reach our destination, up at the top of the Hollywood Hills in a secret grove of eucalyptus trees, where we'd be alone except for the moon and the wind. I'd turn her around, bend her over the seat, and slide those leather jeans over her hips and *down*.

"Down," she said, again pulling me out of my fantasies. "Lie down."

I followed her order immediately, going quickly from my knees to my back on the wooden floor, watching wide-eyed as she straddled my legs and slid down my thighs until she was sitting sex-to-sex on top of me.

She could tell that I was packing, I was sure of it, the synthetic cock pressing at her through two pairs of leather jeans. She could feel the ache of it, wanting her, and she smiled as she reached out and stroked it, stroked *me* through the hide, caressing me. I could tell from her look of ecstasy that I had met my match. Finally, after many years of searching, many more lying in wait, I had found my leather lady.

She didn't touch the button fly, didn't make any move to undo my pants, she only stroked, and teased, and played with me through the worn leather.

But she denied me.

Her hands continued to work, her fingers to dance their intricate steps up and down the crotch of the jeans. Then, without saying a word, she began moving her body forward, taking over from her fingers with her sweet little pussy, rubbing in circles, endless circles of her hips against mine. Around and around. I helped her, grabbing on to her waist and finding that fast, pounding beat. Moving her up and down, then a quick circle, up and down the rigid shaft of the molded cock. Wanting nothing more than to rip open the buttons, tear off her slacks, and slam it into her. But then, wanting anything but to lose the feel of the leather, the softness of it, the slender caress of it tight on us both.

"What do you want?" I managed to whisper, the image of her on my cycle still burning in my head; the feel of her skin where it showed, at her wrists, at the neck of her jacket, at her throat, the bits that I saw inflaming me. The leather of her body, the hide and the hide, engulfing me.

"What do you want?"

If she needed me inside her, I would do that. I would take down her slacks, unbutton my own, and plunge the phallus into the wet heat of her pussy. I could smell that wet heat, knew what it would feel like as it dripped down the plastic dildo and matted against my fur. But if she wanted to come in the leather, come *through* the leather, I'd do that too.

She surprised me.

"Shh, Patrice. Don't say anything. Let me."

In a flash, she was up and grabbing the motorcycle gloves from the edge of my desk. Then she motioned for me to stand and undo my fly. I did it, my fingers slipping only once in their hurry to loose the buttons.

Her gloved hand reached in, took over, freeing the flesh-colored cock and bringing it to her lips. The leather-covered fingertips reached lower, probing, trying to find my cunt beneath the harness. I didn't need her to touch me there, simply watching her mouth around the head of the cock drove me crazy. She worked me hard, worked me well, sliding the cool leather across the feverish skin of my flat belly, bringing me to a boiling point with the inferno of her mouth as she deep-throated the cock and pressed her lips all the way to my body. She knew…she knew everything. The two sensations, skin on skin. The slickness of her glossy lips, then the smooth leather caress, the heat of her tongue trailing lower to tickle my thighs, then the heavy weight of her gloved hand going back between my legs to tickle my asshole.

I stroked her fiery curls while she worked, faster and faster, the glove and her tongue, the leather sliding on the wetness of the cock, the oiled-up feeling as her hand moved piston-fast on the shaft. But then suddenly she settled back on her heels and looked up at me with a mixed expression of lust…and anticipation. I did not let her down.

I drew her to her feet, lifted her into my arms, and brought her to my heavy wooden desk. Quickly, I peeled the gloves from her hands and slid them on my own, delighting in the warmth left by her body heat. Then, just as quickly, I unzipped her leather slacks and pulled them down, only to her thighs, giving me the perfect access to her pussy and asshole. Lovely. Perfect. I parted her ginger-furred kitty lips with two fingers and found her clit, teasing it with my gloved hand, brushing my fingertips against it until she cried out from the intensity.

Then I went to work with my mouth, treating her as she had treated me. My fingers and my tongue. The leather and the love. I could not get enough, tickling her with my thumb and forefinger until her juices ran down the sweet silken slit between her thighs. Then I lapped every drop, breathing in deeply to catch the most haunting woman-smell, musky and sublime, mixed with the scent of the leather, warm, dark. Living.

The combination of it: the smell of her, the taste of her, the mingling scents together had my pussy dripping sweet juices down my thighs. Before she could come, I stood, grabbing her around the waist, and impaled her with the cock, slamming into her, pressing my body hard against hers. Poetry in motion, this time written by yours truly.

Sinful. Dangerous. Wild. Alive.
The skin on the skin. The hide on the hide.

ABOUT THE EDITOR

CALLED A "LITERARY SIREN" by *Good Vibrations*, Alison Tyler is naughty and she knows it. She is the author of more than twenty explicit novels, including *Rumors*, *Tiffany Twisted*, and *With or Without You* (all published by Cheek), and the winner of "best kinky sex scene" as awarded by *Scarlet Magazine*. Her novels and short stories have been translated into Japanese, Dutch, German, Italian, Norwegian, Greek, and Spanish.

According to *Clean Sheets*, "Alison Tyler has introduced readers to some of the hottest contemporary erotica around." And she's done so through the editing of more than thirty-five sexy anthologies, including the erotic alphabet series published by Cleis Press; as well as the *Naughty Stories from A to Z* series, the *Down & Dirty* series, *Naked Erotica*, and *Juicy Erotica* (all from Pretty Things Press). Please drop by www.prettythingspress.com.

Ms. Tyler is loyal to coffee (black), lipstick (red), and tequila (straight). She has tattoos, but no piercings; a wicked tongue, but a quick smile; and bittersweet memories, but no regrets. She believes it won't rain if she doesn't bring an umbrella, prefers hot and dry to cold and wet, and loves to spout her favorite motto: "You can sleep when you're dead." She chooses Led Zeppelin over the Beatles, the Cure over NIN, and the Stones over everyone—yet although she appreciates good rock, she has a pitiful weakness for '80s hair bands. In all things important, she remains faithful to her partner of more than a decade, but she still can't settle on one perfume. Visit www.alisontyler.com for more luscious revelations or myspace.com/alisontyler, if you'd like to be her friend.